Barely aware of what she was about, Nicole shrugged herself into a dress, sat in front of her dressing-table and applied make-up with a heavy hand. Then she stalked back into the living-room and stood in the doorway. 'I'm ready.'

Adam turned towards her, stood for a moment, then was walking across with that imperious stride, lithe and graceful, past her and into her bedroom without a word. Speechless, she followed, not understanding until she saw him throw open the wardrobe door, riffle through the few things on the rail.

'You needn't.' A sob broke through the words. 'I'm not going to change this.' She threw out a hand to indicate her dress. 'What does it matter how I'm dressed?'

'To me it doesn't.' He spoke through clenched teeth and thrust a creamy dress at her. 'But there are others to be considered.'

COUNTERFEIT MARRIAGE

BY

ALEXANDRA SCOTT

MILLS & BOON LIMITED
ETON HOUSE   18-24 PARADISE ROAD
RICHMOND   SURREY   TW9 1SR

First published in Great Britain 1990
by Mills & Boon Limited

© Alexandra Scott 1990

Australian copyright 1990
Philippine copyright 1990
This edition 1990

ISBN 0 263 76901 1

Set in Times Roman 11 on 11½ pt.
01-9012-51931 C

Made and printed in Great Britain

CHAPTER ONE

FROM the corner of her eye Nicole saw him approach. She ignored the slight, inexplicable increase in her heartbeat. What right did *he* have to be here? Who had asked him? She tightened her lips, kept her attention deliberately fixed on Mr Roebuck's face as if she found his long, tedious story spellbinding. The other guests who had been there when he'd set off on his convoluted anecdote about his difference of opinion with the local planning office had drifted away, leaving Nicole with a clear field.

And she was unwilling to hurt her grandfather's old friend—everyone, even Opa knew how boring he could be, but still ... A movement in the mirror opposite made her draw in a sudden nervous breath; the reflection told her that the tall, dark-suited figure, the man she had encountered once or twice without having met, the one who had lingered disturbingly in her memory for a time, had now paused on the fringe of her vision, just by her elbow. Jem Roebuck faltered, paused in mid-flow and looked up, a slight frown clearing as he recognised the newcomer.

'Aha!' He smiled with genuine pleasure. 'So you made it after all. I've just been telling this young lady here...' He inclined his head with the old-fashioned gallantry which made her feel quite ridiculous, more so when she became aware of the flood of colour that swept her cheeks. And still she refused to look at the newcomer, her reasons too complex to analyse. Maybe after all he was merely a guest like the others, assembled for Sunday morning drinks to celebrate her grandparents' forty years of marriage. With an effort she wrenched her thoughts back to Jem. ' . . . about a battle I've just been waging against the planning people. I think I've just about got them . . .'

'Yes, I'm sure.' His voice was deep and mellow, as somehow she had known it would be, and disturbing. That she hadn't expected, and against her own inclination Nicole flicked an upward glance at the newcomer. Confirming what she already knew, what she had known even before he appeared in the drawing-room doorway; that there was something . . . well, magnetic was a corny, overworked word, out of date too, but in this case it seemed to render all other descriptions redundant. In her two previous encounters with him, brief and fleeting though they had been, she had recognised that very quality—something compelling, difficult to dismiss, impossible to identify.

It wasn't so much that he was handsome, though he was good-looking in a strong rugged sort of way, with the kind of shoulders that played forward in rugby, the kind that even immaculately tailored suiting couldn't diminish. He was a tall man, way above six feet, so that she at five feet seven felt quite tiny. Dark hair inclined to fall across his forehead . . . and his eyes—at a distance she had never been able to decide, but now she could see they were intense brown flecked with amber. Striking eyes, impossible to ignore when they were turned in your direction. She moved uneasily under their scrutiny, and her legs felt weak.

For though he was still talking to Jem it was on her that his whole attention was quite firmly focused. Her breath quickened further, and she nibbled her lower lip in frustration as she sought some distraction and found it in the dark maroon tie which picked up the thinnest of overchecks in the three-piece suit he wore, waistcoat buttoned over a white shirt. Utterly, boringly conservative, she decided in an attempt at disparagement.

'I'm sure you'll give them a run for their money.' The stranger had found a crack in Jem's tale and interrupted with suave, practised tact. 'But I was sent over to tell you that your presence is urgently required at the other side of the room.' As he turned to indicate, his eye caught Nicole's, a spark of mischief inviting her to share with him the humour of the situation. 'Walther would like you to arbitrate in a difference of opinion with Robbie.'

'Really?' As Jem swung round, his hand reached out for the glass he had put down on the side table. 'Oh, I see.' He acknowledged his host's look of appeal and nodded. 'Well, it looks as if I'll have to go without letting you know how it all ended. Excuse me, will you? I'll see you before I leave, Nicole.'

'Don't worry about Nicole. I'll look after her.' And to demonstrate that determination the stranger put a hand on her elbow and propelled her in the direction of the french windows which opened on to the terrace. He closed them behind him masterfully, as if he were on home ground and not just a guest in the house.

'Well...' Relieved to escape Jem she might be, but what right did he think he had to...? Besides, she had always hated masterful men—bossy was generally a more apt description. She pulled herself from his grasp and turned with what she hoped was a repressive smile. 'I'm not altogether sure that I want to be looked after.'

'You're not?' The striking eyes widened momentarily, his tone mocking though there was no hint of a smile, or even of the indulgence which in her present mood would have made her long to spit and scratch. 'I thought all women wanted that. Certainly——'

'You're way behind the times, Mr...' She paused, but when he showed no inclination to offer his name she concluded rather lamely, 'You're thinking of the Victorians.'

'Am I?' Now his lips did curl in amusement, the eyes, disturbing, perceptive, seeming intent on recording every pore and line on her face. 'But some attitudes are ageless. I was going to say that most men want to be looked after. The one needn't exclude the other; it's not a sexist issue. In fact——' his amusement increasing, he raised one foot enclosed in highly polished expensive leather on to a low wall and relaxed, leaning forward on to an elbow, chin supported by fingers as he looked round the garden brilliant with flowers before at last coming back to rest on her face '—I would think, if you can find it, it might prove to be the perfect relationship. You need look no further than your grandparents for the ideal example. It's when all the caring is on one side that...' His voice trailed away; his expression changed, grew almost bleak for a moment before he straightened up, but Nicole barely heard that last unfinished comment.

She was staring at him in aggravation, irritated—unduly so, though she didn't pause to consider that—that he knew so much about her family when as far as she knew they had never exchanged a word. Her slender, dark eyebrows came together in concentration. No...she couldn't have. Not even when she was very much younger; she was bound to have remembered. He was not the kind of man you could forget. No matter how hard you tried, it was bound to be impossible.

'But...' She caught herself staring and wrenched at her attention, running her hands down her arms as if she were chilly; indeed, she repressed a shiver. 'I think I'll go inside. It isn't really warm enough out here——'

'Nonsense.' He had, it would appear, the gift of seeing right through her, recognising her motives, finding amusement in them. 'Nonsense.' He came closer, raising a hand and grasping her upper arm in fingers that, while gentle, gave the impression of determined, implacable strength. 'It's as perfect as you're likely to find in the middle of June. And I was hoping, Nicole, that you might feel like showing me round the garden. I'm about to acquire a place in the country and it's time I started picking up some gardening hints. When you've lived most of your life in the city you...'

But only one word registered with her; for all she understood about his place in the country he might as well have been speaking Swahili. Her name. How was it that he could use her name so easily when they hadn't even been introduced? She made an effort and drew away, facing him, hands on hips, staring with the same deliberate challenge he himself employed.

'You seem to know an awful lot about me. How come you know my name when I haven't a clue about yours?'

He looked at her for a long time, then she imagined she saw his lips twitch, a suspicion confirmed by the broad grin which came a moment later. She noticed, while trying not to, that he had strong white teeth, one of the front ones the slightest bit crooked, which seemed to add to his attr... She caught herself up before the thought could register, and in any case his, 'Come off it, Nicole,' made her realise he was challenging her words. She gasped with indignation, but before she could think of a crushing reply he went on, 'The moment I looked through the window in your grandfather's office and saw you running over the tarmac, I made it my business to find out exactly who you were.'

'And so——' she managed to inject her tone with biting scorn '—that makes you certain I did likewise.'

'Well——' he shrugged his shoulders, raised his hands in surrender, though she knew he was still laughing '—one always hopes.'

Torture, she assured herself hotly, would not have forced from her the admission that he was very nearly right. She had quizzed her grandfather's secretary when she had got into the building, only she had not been given a satisfactory answer. For Elsa had been running round like a headless chicken, not hearing what was being said, she was so frantic with worry about a mislaid document. 'No, you cannot see him, he's in conference with some big noises from the States. And they're all in there, waiting for this paper I can't find.' She had been almost crying with frustration, and for some reason Nicole associated the taut, nervy atmosphere with the figure who had watched her from the window.

'Looks as if I called at an awkward time, Elsa. Just tell him I dropped off his calculator; he always says he's lost without it.'

'What?' Elsa had raised her worried face from the filing cabinet. 'Oh, yes, I'll tell him. Not that he'll be bothering, we have too many other things on our plate right now. Oh, thank heavens...' She had pulled out a paper and walked to the inner door, smoothed her hair nervously, and tapped timidly as Nicole turned away. Nicole had been surprised that Elsa felt so uneasy. The older woman's manner added to a certain tetchiness from her normally equable grandfather...she couldn't think why the two were connected, but...

She had made her way along the corridor and popped her head inside the drawing office to have a word with Anne Darling, whom she had known since their first day at Infants' School. Anne had showed off her new engagement ring, they'd discussed the wedding date, and Nicole had left, crossing to the car park and sliding behind the wheel of her sports car.

Then she'd caught sight of Rod Beardsley. He was in charge of the Accounts Department, and was a man she had known most of her life, who had indulgently allowed her to bash out lists of figures on an old adding machine on her occasional invasions of his domain.

He had been standing by the main entrance, talking to someone, and without thinking she had called his name and waved. But Rod had been too immersed in his nervy dissertation to hear; he'd continued to talk, a forefinger punching the air in explanation while his companion swung lazily round on one heel, making her draw in a nervous breath as he stared at her with the same direct intensity he had shown when he had stared through the window of her grandfather's office. And even at that distance he had been able to bring the colour to her cheeks.

Impatiently she had switched on the engine, still only vaguely aware that Rod's usual calm air of being in total command had deserted him; another glance and she'd seen that his face was red, hair disordered, and that he seemed to be talking rather too quickly. His companion was listening, saying nothing, and as she'd driven towards them she'd been well aware of his continuing interest in her.

On impulse—it would be stupid to deny that she was trying to get back at the stranger who seemed to be disrupting all their lives—she had wound down the window, given two authoritative blips on her horn and called brightly, 'Don't let them get you down, Rod!' And she was accelerating away almost as soon as Rod had the chance to recognise her, and certainly without allowing her eyes to admit the presence of that other figure. Only her satisfaction had been short-lived, for he had nagged at her all the way back to town, worrying at the back of her mind for days until gradually she had been absorbed by all that was going on at college...

But now the intervening months simply evaporated, and Nicole was remembering her anger with him, as firm as ever in her certainty that somehow all her grandfather's problems were tied up with this man. His presence here today merely confirmed that. She forced a smile and took a step back, facing him, hands on hips, staring with the same challenge that he adopted so successfully. 'I thought I knew all my grandfather's friends.' She allowed a tiny sardonic inflexion on that word. 'But, as I say, it seems strange that I still don't know who you are, yet you know me.'

'Well——' he appeared not to notice her discouragement '—I've been hearing about you from your grandfather for a good many years now, and in the last six months or so... Well, let's say I know as much about you as any one person has the right to know about another. Until they've been introduced, that is.'

'Then you have the advantage over me.' She would not be seduced by his light-hearted manner. She allowed another wave of furious indignation to envelop her. That this... this stranger should know all about the family skeletons rattling away in their cupboards, while she... It would be easy to allow herself to be overwhelmed by him: he was so different from the men she was used to; older, for one thing, years older than her fellow students. About Justin's age, she decided, glad to have another black mark to set against his name. Name? What name? 'And yet,' she stated as coolly as she could, 'you refuse to tell me who you are.'

'It keeps slipping my mind; I know *you* so well.' Still deliberately mocking and yet...disarming too. 'My name is Randell. Adam Randell.'

The surname meant nothing to her, buried as it was deep in her memory, but the first name— Adam. That leapt instantly into her mind and took her straight back to that stupid conversation she had overheard ages ago... almost nine months— she made a quick calculation—so long ago that its importance had just about faded from her mind. But Adam—Adam Randell. That *was* the name, she would stake her life on it. She ran the tip of her tongue over lips that were suddenly dry, her brain reeling with shock, desperately trying to cope with this wholly unexpected and unwelcome knowledge.

She stared up at him, panic showing before she had a thought of guarding her expression, and something about his look, hooded, secret, confirmed all the suspicions that were racing headlong through her mind. A trickle of ice ran down her spine, and it was with difficulty that she controlled a shiver.

'How do you do?' Her voice was only slightly uncertain. To play it cool, that was the main thing, not to show by the flicker of an eyelid that it meant anything at all. 'I thought I had met all grandfather's *friends*, but it seems I was wrong. Nice to meet you, Mr Randell. But now, would you excuse me? I'm sure they're desperate for help in the kitchen.' Without waiting for a reaction she turned, walking swiftly round the side of the house, through a side door and into the hall, sneaking upstairs, leaning back against her bedroom door for a few moments before going to her dressing-stool and slumping in front of the mirror, one hand pressed to her chest as if she had the means to subdue the agitation.

Adam Randell. She studied herself, decided she could do without the histrionics, and moved her hand to push a troublesome curl of hair back from her forehead. It quite undermined the severely sculptured style she had chosen for today's party. Very difficult and trying to achieve she had found it, too; endless effort in pulling all the hair to the crown and running the thick chestnut plait from forehead to nape. *Not* a fashion likely to become a habit. Opa would be pleased at that; he didn't care for it, thought it was too old for her, but she considered it sophisticated.

The grey eyes were worried, the delicate eyebrows arched in concentration, and for a split second Nicole saw her grandfather's expression. It was true, then, what everyone told her. She grinned suddenly. Surprising but true: she had inherited those long, dark lashes, the perfect frame for her expressive eyes, from dear, stolid Opa. The creamy skin, the full mouth were her grandmother's; she could trace nothing of herself to closer relatives, since she had none.

She waited for the familiar ache to hit her, but instead her mind somersaulted back to what had happened downstairs. Adam Randell... She got up, looked at her reflection in agitation, and ran her open palm over the shapely curve of her bosom, pausing at the narrow waistline and flat stomach. She hoped, prayed Opa and Oma weren't still harbouring that stupid idea, for he wasn't the kind of man... Oh, what was the use? They weren't, after all, living in Victorian times—her mouth twisted wryly at the repetition of the phrase which seemed to be marking the day—and even if they had any idea of trying to...they would never force her...

Nicole took a last look in the long mirror, smoothed the silky black material that clung seductively, swirling and swaying, about her legs as she walked, adjusted the wide bronze-coloured belt, and turned, hurried to the top of the staircase. And she was just in time to see her grandparents close the door on the man who had been having such an unsettling effect.

Thank heavens. Her heart bounded in relief; a weight fell from her and she rushed light-hearted down the last few steps, encompassing them both with an impulsive hug. 'Oma, Opa!' Curious how often the old childhood names for them tripped off her tongue. 'I still can't believe you've been married all those years; you look much too young.' She forced all her worries aside for today.

'*Ja?* You think so?' In celebration of the occasion Opa had had more than his usual quota of wine, and was happy and playful. 'For me is not true, but Friede...' He stopped and looked at his wife admiringly. 'She looks pretty, like the day I married her. No, more pretty. So much more.' He took his wife's hand and raised it to his lips. 'And now, before I forget, Nicky—Adam, you met him, no? He says to tell you he is sorry he had to rush off without saying goodbye.'

'Oh?' Difficult to imagine why such a message should have been necessary.

'Yes, but he says tomorrow he will come and take you out to dinner. That is nice for you...' Just then he caught sight of a departing friend and turned away. Nicole looked at her grandmother with an expression of dismay, a gesture of desperate appeal.

'Gran, I don't want to go out with Adam Randell; why on earth should I?'

'I would have thought most girls would be flattered, Nicole.'

'Most girls. What has that to do with it, Gran? I don't want to go out with him and I won't.' She shook her head stubbornly, decisively, deep down a little surprised that her reaction should be so fiercely negative. 'You can give me his number and I'll ring and tell him. Don't worry, I'll make an excuse, say I have a previous engagement; I don't want to embarrass you or Opa.'

'No?' The old woman sighed and Nicole, looking more intently, recognised the expression of strain that had been coming and going over recent months. 'Well, if you feel like that, Nicky... But try not to upset Opa, will you? He's not been terribly well and...'

'Gran, that isn't fair.'

'Fair?' She looked at her granddaughter steadily for a long moment. 'Fair?' she echoed then smiled very faintly. 'I suppose you're right, Nicky. Maybe it isn't fair.' She turned with a slight smile—and even that seemed to cost an effort—walked forward, and slipped her arm through her husband's in a comforting gesture as they stood saying goodbye to the rest of their guests.

Nicole, disturbed in a vague but intense way, drifted about picking up plates and empty glasses, wishing she could ignore that old conversation now alive in her mind and hammering for attention.

It had been the repetition of her own name that had brought her eyes up from an absorbing novel, to sit for a moment with her head on one side then swing her legs on to the floor with a barely stifled yawn. But she was still enveloped in the curtains which hung in heavy folds from ceiling to floor, effectively isolating the window-seat, for long her favourite retreat.

Not that she had been in retreat that afternoon; she had simply been enjoying the peace and tranquillity of her own home after the wearing enforced togetherness of her school in France. How boring it had been, all the chatter of her contemporaries whose single aim, or so it would seem, was to catch a rich husband as soon as possible, and put to use all those tedious lessons on flower-arranging and making seating plans for dinner parties.

Her own name again. She pushed aside the curtains, about to get to her feet, when she realised quite suddenly that she was eavesdropping. Although the conversation next door revolved round her, it was certainly not intended for her ears.

'Anyway——' her grandparents still spoke with the pronounced accents which over forty years of residence in England had not been able to eliminate and, being slightly deaf, Opa's voice was correspondingly loud '—to me it would be the perfect answer for Nicky to marry Adam. Only then would I feel happy and secure.'

'*Ja,*' Oma agreed, but in the considered, quiet way that was a counterbalance to her husband. 'But you cannot say, Walther; girls these days, they don't marry but to please themselves. Certainly not to make their grandparents happy.'

'What do girls know? It seems the more they marry to please themselves, the more mistakes they make. When the parents chose the husbands for them, how many divorces did we have then, tell me?'

'Not many, Walther.' Listening, Nicole could imagine her grandmother calmly threading a length of tapestry wool through a needle and beginning to pull it through the canvas. 'But now *they* decide, and if they can't be happy they prefer to be miserable alone than in twos. I can't say I blame them.'

'Hmm.' Walther König made the dismissive noise familiar to many of his employees as well as to his family. 'Happy? Happy? What is happy? It's something people think about too much. If you spend your life asking, "Am I happy?" then don't be surprised if many times the answer you get is no. Even me, if I were to keep asking then maybe I would find out I wasn't happy. But I don't ask, so I never find out. I think Adam would be a fine match; you know you agree with me, Friede.'

'I agree, I agree!' Her grandmother sighed deeply as if this was an assurance she was weary of making. 'But it isn't my agreement you have to get, Walther. I told you, girls these days marry for love, and I don't suppose Nicky is any different from the rest of her generation.'

'Love,' the old man grumbled. 'We all know where love gets you.'

A tiny trickle of cold water ran down Nicole's spine. It was clear he was referring to his daughter, their spoiled darling who had suddenly run off with a man no one could approve of, a man who had agreed to marry her with great reluctance just weeks before her baby was due. That, the terrible tension and the worry of it, had brought on a cerebral haemorrhage which had robbed the couple of their daughter and left them with a sickly grandchild to raise, since the father showed less than no interest in her well-being. Nicole shivered, rubbed her hands down bare arms which were all at once goose-pimpled and chilly, then her grandfather spoke again.

'You'll speak to her about it then, Friede?'

'Wouldn't it be better coming from you, Papa? After all, it's your plan, you would explain it better.'

'Maybe, maybe. But do you think it might be better to wait till they meet. Adam is a fine-looking young man; maybe she would fall in love with him and there would be no need to say anything.'

'You think that is likely?' His wife laughed. 'I'm sure marriage is the furthest thing from Nicky's mind. She's still determined to go to college and learn to paint.'

'You never know, it's when people aren't even thinking of it that they can make clear decisions. Look at us, Friede; the last thing on my mind was taking the responsibility of a wife and family, but then you came along...'

Another laugh, scornful and discouraging. 'So far as I can remember, I came along a full year before you proposed.... If you're prepared to give Nicky time to fall in love with him, maybe...'

'*Ach*, no, a year, did you say it was? I doubt Adam will wait that long. No, unless we get the whole thing tied up in the next six months I think he'll turn his eyes elsewhere.' It seemed a long time before his wife spoke again.

'And then what?' Her voice was subdued, sober, all of her natural gaiety wiped away. 'Do you...do you think you could find another buyer for the firm, Walther?'

'We shall have to hope.' Even her grandfather seemed to have lost most of his bounce. 'I doubt if we can ever find anything more beneficial. You know there would be all those written-in benefits for Nicole. And it means a lot that Adam would allow me to stay on and run the factories as a separate entity; anyone else would insist on my retirement and...' his voice shook a little '...what would I do without the business, Friede?'

'Oh, surely, Walther, no one would take that away from you? It's your life, you built it up from nothing when you came here after the war and——'

'It's a long time ago, *liebling*.' He sighed. 'I'm getting old. Is it time maybe I was thinking of taking a back seat? Anyway, you're probably right, Friede, and it wouldn't be right to ask the child to marry for the sake of the business. Although——' his voice strengthened '—I still think such a marriage would have as much chance of success as any other.' His footsteps could just be heard on the thick carpet as he walked to the hall door. 'Love,' he scoffed amiably. 'What sense is there in marrying for a reason like that?'

As the words faded Nicole could hear the door closing, then the sound of her grandmother crossing to the kitchen, footsteps echoing on the tiled floor. She released a sigh, deep and shuddering, curling her legs beneath her as she burrowed more closely into the cushioned window-seat. The book, totally absorbing a moment before, lay where it had fallen on the floor. It was true, then: eavesdroppers were unlikely to hear anything to their advantage. She had told her grandmother she was going for a walk so there was no use blaming them for talking so freely; they thought they had the house to themselves, after all.

Damn it all. She pressed an agitated hand to her forehead. If she was reading things correctly, her grandfather was having business difficulties and was hoping that her marriage to someone called Adam Randell would solve those problems. What the dickens was she to do?

She would do anything for her grandparents. Anything. And she couldn't bear to think of Opa being so worried. She knew how much his small group of factories meant to him, could hardly imagine him deprived of the purpose they gave to his life. Anything she could do for them, or almost anything...but surely she had misunderstood in some way; they couldn't possibly mean what she thought she heard. Not...not marriage. She wasn't *nearly* ready...

Silently she got to her feet, pushed open the window and swung her legs over the sill. She would make a wide sweep of the garden and come towards the back of the house as if she had really been for a walk across the common. The last thing she wanted was for them to suspect that their conversation had been overheard; she must have time to think things out before embarking on any kind of discussion.

Through the kitchen window she could see her grandmother's head bent over a bowl, beating at a mixture with a tireless arm. Nicole opened the door and went inside, wiping her feet carefully on the mat before venturing on to the sparkling blue and white tiles.

'You look busy, Oma.' She crossed and stood for a moment as the operation continued. 'What are you making?'

'Potato pancakes.' The arm didn't falter or flag in its rhythmic motion.

'Oma.' Nicole laughed, put her arm round the old woman's waist and gave an affectionate squeeze. 'Why don't you use the mixer Opa gave you? You know it would save a lot of hard work.'

'That's true,' she smiled, allowing herself a moment's respite to draw breath before she began again, 'but I don't think it makes such good pancakes.'

'We ought to have a proper test some day. Make two lots, one in the mixer, the other by hand, see if we can tell the difference when they're cooked.'

'I don't think so.' Oma smiled, pursing her lips as she reached for the heavy skillet to place on the hotplate. 'I might not like the result.'

'Oh, Gran, what on earth do you mean? If they were just as good from the mixer, think of the time you would save.'

'That's what I mean.' Methodically, unhurriedly, the old woman crossed the kitchen to the refrigerator and returned with her carefully hoarded crock of goose fat, a little of which she used to grease the skillet. 'Why is everyone so anxious to save time nowadays?'

'I don't know, Gran.' Nicole's shrug admitted defeat. 'Maybe you have a point.'

She watched her grandmother drop spoonfuls of the mixture on to the sizzling griddle, noting the deft flattening action with the back of the spoon, the patience with which she stood watching them cook.

'Yes.' She turned away for a moment, setting three plates on the scrubbed wood table, arranging forks and knives, going back to the stove just as the pancakes were ready for turning. 'When I was young people didn't think so much about saving time. They did what was necessary and if there was a little time to spare at the end of the day they were grateful. Now, go into the workshop and tell Opa;

he loves potato pancakes and it's a long time since
I made them for him.'

'He says he's just coming.' When she returned
Nicole felt depressed. She had just remembered how
potato pancakes had a habit of appearing in times
of stress. Last time had been when that letter had
arrived out of the blue from the States. It had been
from her father inviting her out to visit him and
his American wife. And for a few days it seemed
they had eaten little else but pancakes.

'Sit down, child.' Expertly her grandmother
placed two nicely browned pancakes on one of the
plates. 'There's no saying when Opa will appear.
"Just coming" can mean anything. When he has
some new development on his mind he forgets
everything else.'

'They're delicious, Gran.' Nicole broke off a
piece with a fork and munched. 'Hot,' she warned
as her grandmother sat opposite and began to eat.
'I think you must be right about making them the
hard way; the machine wouldn't make them nearly
as well.' She turned as the door opened and her
grandfather came in, crossing to the sink to wash
his hands. 'Just in time, Opa.' Her grandmother
got up, came back with a loaded plate and began
to serve them. 'No, Gran. I daren't.'

'Daren't?' The glance was of amazement. 'What
can you mean, Nicole?'

'I mean,' she eased a finger round the waistband
of her jeans, 'I don't want to put on any more
weight.'

'Oh, that.' Oma put another pancake on to the
plate. 'Potato pancakes won't put on an extra
ounce. All the books say so now: potatoes won't
put on fat. Five years ago the potato was blamed

for everything but now, is so good for you. I know all along, of course, so...always make potato pancakes.'

'I've been thinking, Oma...' Now seemed as good a time as any to broach the matter of her future. 'And you too, Opa.' They seemed disinclined for the moment to let her in on their plans, so maybe a nudge in the right direction would concentrate their minds. 'I've more or less decided to take up that option and go to art college after all...' Her voice trailed away as the stunned silence seemed to grow tangible. The old man stopped eating, his loaded fork halfway to his open mouth. Oma simply sat and stared. 'I think it's the best plan, don't you?' Nervousness caused her voice to rise a little. 'Best to get a decent education, then...'

'Art college.' It was Oma who spoke first and only after she and her husband had exchanged shocked glances. 'But I thought...last year you decided you would not go to university; I thought...that was why we sent you to France, to learn the language—to that expensive school,' she added as an afterthought.

'Yes, well, I'm sorry about that.' Now that she knew something of the true position she really did feel sorry, but at the time she had had no idea that money was less plentiful than it had always been. And it had been their idea, after all; she had gone to please them. 'But I've given it a lot of thought, and really, what I'm most interested in is to develop my skills in drawing and painting. I know I could have gone to university, but honestly, I just scraped in, and while I was in France, going round all those galleries, that was the only thing that excited me, seeing all those wonderful Impressionist paintings. I'd like to earn my living that way.'

'Nicole——' at last her grandfather began to eat the pancakes on his plate, but slowly and with a complete lack of appetite '—have you any idea how difficult it is to earn a living that way? It seems to me the only time an artist earns money is when he is long dead. Then, I agree with you, the amounts his pictures raise are just haywire. But while he's alive he starves in garret. Yes.' He regarded his granddaughter's smile with indignation. 'Is true,' he insisted. 'Is true.' He held out his plate and allowed his wife to refill it. 'The only famous painter is dead one.' He laughed briefly and with a hint of bitterness. 'Easier to earn a living with the scrubbing brush than paintbrush.'

'But I can try.' Nicole had long been able to twist her grandfather round her finger, and she reached out and caught his hand, squeezing it. 'Let me try, Opa. I'm sure to get a grant, so I won't be a drain on you and Oma.'

'Drain?' He scowled and looked at her intently. 'Who say anything about drain? Did you, Oma?' She signalled innocence with a shake of her head. 'Did I say anything about drain?'

'No, of course not. Neither you nor Oma has ever said anything like that, but nevertheless...most girls of my age are expected to support themselves. Even the Princess of Wales.' She appealed to his intense admiration for and loyalty to the Royal Family. 'Wasn't she working, supporting herself before she married Prince Charles? If she can do it, then——'

'Art college?' He speared the last piece of pancake and transferred it to his mouth. 'Very

good, Friede. Excellent pancakes. Art college.'
Clearly his opinion of such institutions had been
formed by some of the wilder reports of the sixties
and seventies. 'Would that mean living...in
London?' It was as if she were suggesting emi-
gration to Sodom, taking a package tour to
Gomorrah.

'Y...yes.' She could think of little to add. It was
while her mother had been living in the capital that
she had met Peter Minter, had returned home six
months pregnant and without a wedding ring.

'Well, then——' Her grandfather pushed back his
chair, wiped his mouth with the blue and white
napkin before getting slowly to his feet. 'We'll have
to think about it, eh, Oma?' Nicole intercepted
another significant glance between the two. 'We'll
think about it.' He left, closing the door quietly
behind him, and his wife sighed deeply as she
munched on a piece of pancake...

Well, that had been nearly nine months ago, just
before she had taken up her place at college, and
the incident had drifted almost forgotten to the back
of her mind. Until now. It was true there had been
one or two pointers to the continuing business
worries—an economy here, a cutback there—but
things hadn't reached a desperate stage and Nicole
had half convinced herself that in a dreamy state
she had put quite the wrong interpretation on the
overheard conversation. But anyway...now that
she was more or less embarked on career training
she was convinced she was on the right path for
her, and there was no way she would even think of
anything as constricting as marriage, so there was

no point in accepting Adam Randell's invitation to dinner.

Even the following evening, sitting in front of her dressing-table mirror while she applied a touch of plum colour to her eyelids and smeared her lips with translucent gloss, Nicole couldn't really explain to herself why she was going. Just that Opa had been so anxious, pleading almost in a way that was so unlike him, and maybe it would be easier to explain face to face that marriage simply wasn't on the cards for her. Although how—she leaned forward, touching mascara to lashes long and dark enough already—just how did you tell a man you weren't going to marry him unless he brought the subject up first? Well, that was one she would have to work out when the time came, think on her feet . . .

'Nicky?' There was a tap on the door and her grandmother's head appeared. 'He is here. Adam . . .'

'I'm coming.' She reached across the bed for her bag, and some appeal in the older woman's expression made her turn round to show off the dark, shimmery swirl of green about her legs. 'Like the dress, Gran?' She hadn't meant to wear anything so becoming, nor to do her face with such care, nor . . .

'It looks beautiful. But then,' she came close and put an affectionate arm about the slender waist, holding her close for a moment, 'how could the *dress* look anything else?'

'Gran! You know I've told you I can't stand flattery.'

'You must be the first woman, then.' Her grandmother smiled conspiratorially, then hustled her

towards the door. 'Anyway——' they walked down
the flight of steps to the hall and her voice dropped
to a whisper '—I'm sure Adam will be telling you
the very same thing.'

Nicole felt the colour blaze in her face when she
looked across into the sardonic expression of her
escort. It was so easy to imagine he was aware of
her reluctance and amused by it. He was talking to
her grandfather as they stood by the door which
led into the conservatory, but all the while his
concentrated attention was on the slim figure
walking towards him. He acknowledged her with
an inclination of the head and a smile. That at-
tractive smile, with a slow crinkling of the eyes,
and Nicole, who had always been susceptible to
warmth, felt a tiny *frisson*, a warning that she must
remember to be on her guard.

He was taller than her memory of him—she determined to be clinical, detached—dark trousers,
she noted, white shirt, checked jacket, casual, elegant, very Giorgio Armani and light years away
from the style of her usual dates. On the other hand,
a tiny thread of prejudice crept in to point out, it
was impossible to pretend he wouldn't be likely to
attract attention, especially the female variety,
wherever he went. Another throb, disconcerting,
totally unwelcome, struck her, and . . .

'Hi.' At last her grandfather stopped talking and
he was able to get a word in. And his eyes, with an
admiring flick from the swathe of gleaming chestnut
hair to the tips of her dark patent shoes, said a
whole lot more.

'Good evening.' The formality was deliberate, the
kind that would have made the men she met during
the week hoot with laughter and put a mocking

hand to her forehead to check for fever. It pleased her to put Adam Randell into a different category, older, stodgier, and besides, she was determined he would get the message that she was an unwilling victim. 'Shall we go?'

He raised an eyebrow, amused rather than irritated by her manner, but it was her grandfather who spoke. 'Yes, off you go, you young people, go off and enjoy yourselves. We shall be in bed when you get back, but Nicole, you will bring in Adam for a drink.'

'I doubt if he'll want a drink. Not if he's driving.' Her tone was bright, very nearly pert.

'A *drink*.' Her grandfather was seldom impatient with her, which made it all the more noticeable when he was. 'Coffee or tea or something. Oma will have some coffee ground and ready, is that not so, Friede?'

His wife smiled. 'Off you go and enjoy yourselves.'

Nicole didn't speak till she had been carefully settled into the car and he had taken his seat behind the wheel, pausing to check her safety-belt was secure.

'You needn't act as if I'm delicate china, you know.' Her tone was edgy, abrasive. 'I'm quite capable of looking after myself. I do it all the time when I'm at college, for heaven's sake.'

There was no answer till they had negotiated the drive and were accelerating along the top road. 'That was mainly for your grandfather's benefit. He does resemble a mother hen the way he clucks after you.' His mildness might have been designed to annoy.

'I haven't noticed.' A lie; often she had been irritated by the old man's obsessively protective manner, had resented it while struggling to hide her feelings.

'Mmm.' He drove the large sleek car with flair and style, as she would have expected, for he was the kind of man who would do most things well, with a combination of assurance and ability which would always guarantee him a head start. 'Your grandfather tends to give the impression that you are the most important thing in his life.'

'After the factories, of course.' Stupid thing to say.

'Maybe.' If she had been fishing for compliments then he wasn't in the mood to indulge her, and she was happy to let the conversation die until he turned in through impressive stone gates and drew up in front of what looked like a private country house.

'Mmm.' She sat for a moment enjoying the clean, classical lines. 'I had no idea this place existed.'

'No reason why you should. It's been going just a couple of years, a very private private club. Closed to non-members.'

Certainly it was an impressive example of restrained luxury. They were met at the door and ushered into a small sitting-room where several other guests were sipping drinks and poring over menus. Chintz-covered sofas were drawn round a blazing log fire, and tall windows gave a view of the extensive park. Nicole stood for a moment looking towards the small lake, at the swans gliding with elegant detachment over the mirrored surface, white feathers gilded by the setting sun.

'Mmm.' What could one do but approve such perfection? 'How lovely.'

'What will you have to drink, Nicole?'

'Something long and cool. Maybe lime and soda with masses of ice, if that's possible.' She was mildly surprised when she heard him order low-alcohol lager, almost resentful of her deep-down approval, wanting nothing to interfere with her determination to be at odds with this man. And to show it. Politely, of course.

It was pleasant to sit back and relax; she listened to his account of a particularly trying flight he had made to Los Angeles recently, when his luggage had been misdirected twice before turning up as he was about to leave on the return trip. He told the story crisply, with a wry grin at his own inadequacies, making her laugh out loud several times when she forgot to keep the purpose of this outing right at the forefront of her mind. It would be so easy...

And he continued to amuse her while they were eating; she was laughing in spite of all her determination. She withdrew a little, then was disconcerted by his knowing, quizzical expression.

'But that's enough about me. I'm hogging the conversation; my friends complain about it all the time. Tell me about you, Nicole.'

'I thought you knew all about me.' Her tone was deliberately evasive, sharper than even she intended.

'I know a bit from your grandfather's point of view.' He nodded at the waiter who had come forward to refill their glasses. 'Not a lot about the real Nicole.'

'The real Nicole.' She appeared to consider. 'Very little to tell, really. I expect you know I'm studying art.' She flicked up her lashes and was thrown by the expression in his eyes. Lively, interested almost . . . admiring—was that possible? And she was still more disconcerted by her own responses, a throb of pure awareness in the pit of her stomach, an indrawn shuddering breath almost immediately expelled, a light laugh which was nothing less than an effort to conceal her unexpected nerviness. 'Almost a mature student.'

'Really?' Now his eyes truly did sparkle with amused disbelief, widening then narrowing appreciatively. His lips curved as he raised his glass, paused without drinking as he looked at her over the rim. And she was blisteringly aware of so many details. Aware and disturbed by the brown skin of his hands, long fingers circling the stem of the glass, the scatter of dark hair. Long, sensitive fingers, she could so easily imagine . . .

Panic-stricken, she snatched up her own glass, gulping at the wine. With an effort at self-control she set it down with great deliberation on the white cloth, staring down at it, gathering herself together before she found the strength to raise her eyelids and look straight a him. And still it wasn't easy; she forced herself to take several deep breaths, to straighten her back, nervous that her purpose would falter, that she would weaken. There was something . . . something about the way his eyes followed the drift of her hair, moved to her mouth—she found it frightening. A throb of sheer anger stabbed through her. He had no right, it wasn't fair of him to . . . There was a feeling of weakness in her stomach, but really she must; now was the time to stop all this . . . If only she could get rid of this awful ache in her chest. All she wanted was to feel she had done the best she could for her grandparents, that she had tried to relieve them of the terrible anxiety that had been dogging them for so long. If she could do that, then she could put it all to one side and get on with her own life. It had been so difficult recently; just when at last she had been getting over her involvement with Justin, this had to blow up. She straightened her shoulders. 'You know, truly there's no point in all this.' With an effort she looked away from him across the comfortably crowded room, wishing he wouldn't continue to study her with that narrowed yet curiously detached expression. 'It's the most awful waste of your time.'

'Dessert, *mademoiselle*?' Unnoticed, a waiter had pushed a trolley close to her elbow. A silver serving spoon was poised above a crystal bowl as he awaited instructions.

'I don't know.' She resented the interruption, which came at the worst possible moment, when she felt that the slightest touch would push her over the brink. After gearing herself up, now she was being asked the most stupid question about a pudding. When the whole of her future was at stake. She barely glanced at the exotic display before shaking her head decisively. 'No, I won't, thank you.'

'Of course you will.' Adam Randell discounted her wishes. 'Look at those luscious strawberries or figs, how about those? Or ... syllabub or ... some kind of meringue?'

'Vacherin, *monsieur*.'

'Yes, I'll have some of that.' The easiest way of getting rid of him was to take something from his damned trolley and then she might get back to her sole reason for being here.

'And I'll have the figs.' When the man had gone she ate a mouthful or two of the delicious concoction, thin layers of meringue and subtly flavoured creams, and was sliding another sliver to her mouth when he spoke again. 'You were saying...this is an awful waste of time—would...?'

'Your time, I said.' She put down her fork, wiped her mouth with her napkin and sat back, trying to pretend that her heart wasn't playing a wild tattoo against her ribs. 'An awful waste of your time.' The look on his face was disquieting; the flash in the unusual eyes might have been anger. 'Not mine,' she added, with a hint of apology which was a mistake.

'My time?' He detached one of the fan-shaped slices of fruit from the stem, and ate it slowly. 'I'm still not with you, I'm afraid.'

'Oh, don't let's pretend.' The words broke out with more force than she had intended; she intercepted a curious glance from a nearby table and sat forward on the edge of her seat, lowering her voice but speaking with the same passion. 'We both know why you brought me here this evening. All I'm saying is that as far as your plans, yours and grandfather's, are concerned, then it's all for nothing.'

'I see.' His face was impassive. Narrowed eyes were studying her but now they were blank, devoid of any expression which might convey a hint of his reactions. She saw him raise a hand and snap it in the direction of a hovering waiter, saw him scrawl his name on a piece of paper, then, before she was aware of what was happening, she found herself being ushered out to the car, her longish skirt swept inside and the door slammed.

'Now——' for a moment before he switched on the engine he sat looking at her averted profile '—I think it might be a good idea to take up your grandmother's offer of coffee. Then you can tell me exactly what you mean.'

That brought her head jerking round to his. For a moment his eyes were disturbing, hostile, his profile when he started the engine sombre and vaguely threatening. Only by pressing her finger-nails hard into the palms of her hands was Nicole able to retain control; her mind was in a whirl and she was again half convinced that she had made a hideous mistake. Could she possibly have dreamt the conversation which had suggested an arranged marriage between the two of them? Had something in the book she had been reading made her imagination take off, go wild? And . . . if that was the case, how on earth was she going to explain herself? She could just about imagine the contemptuous amusement, the sardonic raised eyebrow. 'Marriage?' The word would be repeated disbelievingly. 'Now what on earth gave you such an idea? And even if there were a vestige of truth in it, what makes you think your name would spring to mind? Eh?'

And she would sit there feeling hideously embarrassed, wishing the floor would open up and swallow her. Unless . . . could she hit on some other reason which would explain her stupid behaviour? But she couldn't. Her brain remained obstinately blank, devoid of any brilliant solutions to this problem of her own engineering.

The car turned into the drive, drove up the incline to the front door. Nicole felt her agitation increase; her heart was hammering loudly against her ribcage and she stared in consternation at the familiar front door.

'Looks as if your grandparents have gone to bed.' He nodded in the direction of the lights in some of the upstairs windows. 'That's good, we needn't worry about interruptions.' A moment later he was holding the car door wide, just like the spider inviting the fly into his parlour. Nicole swung her feet out on to the ground and stood up, determined not to allow her panic to run out of control. She had the distinct impression that, as spiders went, he was likely to be one of the more venomous species.

CHAPTER TWO

ADAM followed Nicole into the kitchen very much as if he felt entirely at home in the house, lounging in the doorway while she filled the kettle, watching so intently that she felt quite nervous as she pushed the pot on to the aga and reached for the can of coffee which her grandmother kept handy. Couldn't he for heaven's sake look somewhere else, admire the view if he felt he had to stare at something?

'Shall we go into the sitting-room?' When it was ready she poured the fragrant brew into cups and handed one to him, offering sugar and cream which he refused, adding a little sugar to her own.

'We'll be comfortable enough here.' He walked forward, hooking a chair with his foot, pulling it out from the table and then sitting, stretching and crossing his long legs. 'You know——' he sipped from his cup then glanced approvingly round the large room '——I've always liked this house. Especially the kitchen. Unusual in a modern place to find a kitchen combining the old and the new so happily. How old is it, do you know?'

'Just over twenty years old.' No difficulty in remembering that. The house had been in its final stages of building when Liese had returned home to have her baby.

'Mmm. I thought about that.'

'They...' Her voice trembled only a little. 'It's rather German in style. What Oma and Opa remembered from the times when they were young.

But I agree with you. I love this old kitchen.' She looked approvingly about her, at the solid dark oak cupboards, traditional blue and white tiles on the walls, then she passed a hand over the scrubbed wood table. 'I always think of it as old.'

'But now——' He drained his cup, rose and went to replenish it from the pot on the aga. She shook her head when he offered her some more. 'Now——' as he took his seat again his eyes swept over her with a disturbing perceptive glance '—let's get back to the subject you brought up back there.' He jerked his head towards the window. 'Something about my time being wasted, wasn't it? Perhaps now you would care to explain.'

She felt the colour come and go in her cheeks. What on earth had possessed her? She had got the entire thing wrong, she knew that now, and she shook her head, praying he would accept her denial and just go away. She didn't think she could cope with the situation much longer, and... 'I think I might have made a mistake. It...'

'A mistake, eh?' He shook his head disbelievingly, a faint smile on his lips. 'I won't buy that, Nicole. And what's more——' He raised his cup and drank, all the while eyeing her over the rim, doubtless noticing and enjoying her tortured embarrassment. 'What's more——' he replaced the cup in the saucer and leaned forward on his elbows '—I think I can make a pretty good guess as to what was going through your mind at that very moment.'

'You can?' Her eyes were wide with astonishment.

'Yes, I think so. Somehow, though I can't explain exactly how, you've got wind of your grandfather's problems and your involvement in them. Am I right so far?'

She nodded without speaking, her eyes riveted on his face.

'And you've heard a rumour that I'll take over the business and all the bad debts only if I can have Walther's granddaughter thrown in as a make-weight. Right?'

'Well...' Why should she feel aggrieved at his way of putting it when basically he had got it just about right? 'Well, yes, I suppose so.'

'I thought that was what was in your mind.' He smiled suddenly in that disconcerting way she found bewildering and unsettling. 'And what makes you think, Nicole, that I have any interest in your...' he allowed his eyes to drift from her face, down over the creamy skin of her neck, lingering over the full curves under the clinging silky material of her dress, then moving smoothly back to her blazing, indignant face '...in your undoubted charms? At least to the extent of taking you for my wife?'

'You haven't?' She released a shuddering sigh that was ninety per cent relief, only ten per cent chagrin. If only he knew how she had to fight off some of the more persistently hopeful of her fellow students—and Justin, she added with a hint of complacency—he might not be so damned patronising, but... 'Well, thank goodness for that.' She got up and reached for his cup, taking it with hers to the sink where she began to rinse them. Surely he would take the hint that the evening was over, that there was no reason for him to put off——?

'Only,' Adam Randell broke into her thoughts, 'it's not quite as simple as that.' Her fingers, busy with the drying towel, paused, and she looked carefully at his face, although now, perversely, he seemed disinclined to look directly at her. 'Unfortunately.'

'Wh . . . what do you mean?'

'What I mean is this.' He rose, crossed the room, paused before swinging round to look at her intently. 'A long time ago, your grandfather tied up most of his capital in a trust fund for you. It's a hideously complicated arrangement and I can't pretend I'm impressed with the legal advice he was given at that time. But anyway, that's what he did and I'm sure he had his reasons. He was determined that no one else would get his hands on his money.' He paused and Nicole knew he was thinking of her father and of Opa's determination that nothing of his would ever fall into Peter Minter's hands. She was angry, angry with Adam Randell for knowing so much of what was so intensely personal and private, but the voice went on inexorably, 'There were all kinds of in-built safeguards to protect your inheritance, and now, when it would have been extremely beneficial for him to have a free hand in using the assets, he finds himself completely hamstrung by his own legal minefield. If that's not a mixed metaphor.' He smiled faintly but she didn't respond; she wasn't remotely in the mood to be amused. 'You know they're in deep water financially.'

'I know things are less rosy than they were.'

'Worse than that, I'm afraid.' He paused; she had the impression he was unwilling to reveal the true scale of the problems as he went on slowly, 'It's been catching up for a long time. Nearly a year ago we wanted to buy him out but there was the stumbling block of your position; he refused to concede anything that might affect you adversely and he decided to hold on in the hope of improvement. That didn't happen, of course; rumours began to circulate which weakened his position still further, so now it's a case of selling out. To me, if he's lucky; I'll offer a good price and he can stay on the board for as long as he wishes. But...'

'But...?' By this time panic was overwhelming her. She couldn't begin to imagine how it would be if her grandfather lost his business...what would he and Oma do? The pain in her chest was just a faint indication of how terrible it would be for them. 'Surely things can't be as bad as that?' Her eyes were wide, a blatant appeal for reassurance.

He looked without speaking, his silence confirming her worst fears. And she refused to read sympathy into that expression. The stoat felt none for the rabbit, did he?

'Then I'll sign something. Anything. Give up all my rights. After all, I've done nothing to merit it; the rewards of all his hard work and——'

'Can't be done, I'm afraid. As I said, the legal knots were tied so firmly they can't be undone. Only... *only* the man you marry will have some control; that will continue until you reach the age of thirty but even that is subject to the approval of your grandparents. Walther has retained some voting rights on that, wisely, in my opinion. If they disagree with your choice of husband then binding constraints come into force which will remain till your thirtieth birthday, and if you don't marry you still have to wait that length of time to come into full control. As I said, it's all highly complicated.

I've had our own legal advisors go through the agreement with a magnifying glass but they can see no way out except with your co-operation.'

'But——' it was a wail of sheer despair '—I've no intention... I'm not going to marry for years. If ever. I have a whole career to fit in before I tie myself down, and I hate the thought——' She bit off the words that would reveal to him her reluctance to trust men. All her life she had been trying to come to terms with her father's rejection, and that was even before she met Justin... Justin Booth, her college tutor, who had made such a big play for her in her first weeks of college that she had come very close to slipping over the edge... And he hadn't thought to hint that he had a wife and family hidden away in the suburbs; that piece of information she had heard quite by chance. No. Men...most men at least—there were a few around honourable as her grandfather—were to be treated with more than a hint of cynical scepticism... Her mind reared away from that unproductive line and returned to what was of pressing importance. She began again, her voice rising in line with her panic and anger. 'I can't and I won't...'

'Don't get too uptight about it all.' He levered himself away from the wall and came a step or two closer. For an instant she had the idea that he might put out a hand to touch her and she shrank away, irrationally pleased when she saw him frown, his eyes glittering dangerously.

'Uptight!' She jumped a further octave. '*Uptight?* Do you expect me to feel calm about it all? How can anyone feel detached about a situation like this? It's more like something out of Jane Austen than something happening here and now.

How can I possibly feel calm?' Her eyes sparked furiously in his direction.

'I think . . . if you could make an effort, try being cool and detached, that might help you to reach a more . . . considered decision.'

'It's so easy to talk; if——'

'I didn't say it was easy. I'm sure it's not easy; worthwhile things rarely are. All I'm saying is, try to take a longer-term view. After all, whatever you decide will have very long-term effects one way or another, and I'm certainly not trying to persuade you. If you do make the wrong decision, you are the one who will have to live with the results. So it's worth making a considered judgement.'

'But it's not the kind of thing that should be considered, is it? Getting married, I mean . . . it's not like . . .' She moved away, paced across the kitchen and turned, beating her tightly clenched fists in the air as a measure of her frustration. 'It's not like going into the market and buying commodities, is it? Or——'

'Not for you, perhaps.' He cut across what she was saying, telling her just how naïve and juvenile her views were, stood there looking at her, a frown making him seem more sombre and vaguely threatening, certainly damaging her self-confidence. 'But for your grandfather and any prospective buyer that is very much what it is like. The chance to save his investment.'

'Well, it's nothing to do with me.' Tears were pricking at the back of her eyes as she made the denial. 'I don't know why I should be sacrificed because he has made a mess of his business.' She was as disgusted with her treachery as he must——

'Don't talk like that.' The harsh, angry voice was instant criticism. 'You haven't a clue, have you? No idea what people like your grandparents went through, no understanding or interest in the efforts they made to pull themselves up by their boot-straps, to make life better for themselves, for their family. Can you imagine what it was like to be thrown up in a strange country without a word of the language, nothing but the clothes on their backs? Of course you can't; you've been sheltered and protected from the day you were born.'

She turned angrily away from his contempt and condemnation but the words continued remorse-lessly, would not be shut out. 'And to end up with this.' From the corner of her eye she saw his arm raised to encompass the kitchen which, with its quiet, solid luxury, epitomised their life, and at once she felt sick with shame.

Of course she knew what he meant. As a child, hadn't she begged time and again to be told the story of how Oma and Opa had made their sep-arate ways across a war-ravaged continent to their new life in a new country. Then it had been told like a romantic fairy-tale, but since growing up she had come to understand the true horror of their lives and the almost miraculous way they had pro-gressed. Though deep down she was well aware that divine intervention had nothing to do with it, their success was a direct result of hard work and deter-mination. For years they had lived in a single room, sharing kitchen and toilet with several other fam-ilies; her grandmother had worked a twelve-hour day in the tiny workshop alongside her husband, stopping for just a week while her baby was born, then taking the child back to work with her. He was quite right, people of her generation didn't know the meaning of hard work, but still... She could have screamed with sheer frustration, but choked down her feelings so only a sobbing sigh escaped her.

'I'm sorry.' Conscious of his eyes, cool now that they had lost their mellow warmth, the light of admiration she had seen early on quite faded, she stared down into an empty coffee-cup as if it might hold some kind of solution to her problem. The silence lengthened till at last she forced the words out. 'You're right, I owe them everything.'

'That isn't what I said.' His voice was only marginally softer. 'But no matter. To get back to the main subject, the fact is, I'm not exactly in a marrying frame of mind either, but on the other hand it is important for me to add your grandfather's companies to my holdings, and if marrying you is the only way of gaining control I'm prepared to consider it at least.'

'But——'

He interrupted before she had the chance to make a point. 'I'm a bit older than you, and I dare say I have learned more, in a harder school... I've always known life is a series of compromises. We can't always have exactly what we want in life, and——'

'I *do* know that.' His implication that she had had a life of total indulgence riled her, and she wasn't prepared to be denied her say. Stormy grey eyes blazed at him across the table. 'But I think most people would draw the line at marriage. I don't know how a man in your position——' her eyes accused him, '—with everything in the world, should have to consider marriage to gain control of a few tuppeny ha'penny companies.'

'Don't,' he cut in icily. 'Don't diminish the König companies, Nicole. You'd be making a mistake if you did. They may have slipped a bit in recent years, but that's largely due to others manipulating the market, and maybe your grandfather isn't quite as astute as he used to be on these matters. Life was gentler when he started out, but now . . . it's dog eat dog out there, and I'm not prepared to see someone like Walther being swallowed up.' His narrowed eyes gave the impression of looking way beyond the immediate subject of discussion. 'Besides, I don't much care for the ethics—the business ethics,' he put in as if to clarify an important point, 'of the opposition.'

This time the silence was prolonged, and Nicole felt her mind go totally blank. It was difficult to accept that this was happening to her, that Nicole Minter was in this ridiculous, surreal situation, the innocent maiden in some stupid Victorian melodrama, being pushed into marriage with a total stranger and . . . and one she wasn't sure she even liked, for heaven's sake! The instant that thought came into her head she heard herself express it.

'Like each other?' He had gone to stand at the window, looking out over the darkening garden, seemingly fascinated by the dark outline of trees against the sky, but he swung round to face her, shoulders in the dark jacket slightly hunched, hands thrust deep into his trouser pockets. For a split second she could have sworn he was amused, but there was little sign of that on his face as he spoke. 'Certainly I don't think I'd have any problems in that direction, but of course I agree it might be more difficult for you.' His self-derision was mellow, tolerant.

Nicole felt herself blush. For no reason which allowed logical explanation, colour and heat raced through her body; her mouth felt tinder-dry yet her palms were damp. Angry with herself, she turned away, collected the coffee-pot from the stove and walked to the sink, brushing against him as she did so.

'The whole thing is ridiculous. For one thing, I'm not ready for marriage. I don't know if I ever will be. Anyway...I've always thought any girl who marries before twenty-five is a complete idiot. Besides...' the unfairness of it struck her with renewed force '...I want to be a painter.' It was an appeal for understanding; she looked at him, wide-eyed, and was met by an expression that was far from reassuring. 'It's what I've always wanted. I want to earn my own living.'

'So?' Guarded though they were, the tawny eyes exerted a powerful influence, and it was difficult for her to look elsewhere. 'I can't see how marriage would change that.'

'Of course it would.' She heard herself being childish, the very antithesis of the sophisticated woman and dedicated artist she would have liked him to see. Tears were very close to the surface and trembled in her voice. 'Of course it would,' she repeated more steadily after a moment. 'How could it be otherwise?'

'You know, I have a flat very close to the college.' His voice held a hint of persuasiveness which put her instincts on the defensive. 'I can see no earthly reason why you shouldn't be able to continue your studies if——'

'But why should I? None of the other students is married. Why should I be the only one? We're all young and carefree, we enjoy life and...'

He did laugh then, openly and with a delight which she had to work hard to resist. 'So?' Still more disturbingly, he reached out towards her; she felt his fingers loop in her hair and for a moment she held her breath, waiting to be pulled against him. She could look nowhere but at his firm, smiling mouth, terrified at the thought of it touching hers and yet excited... Her heart was beating in loud, agitated strokes against her chest even when the pressure was withdrawn, the danger passed. 'So you think that the moment the ring is slipped on to the finger all pleasure is a thing of the past? Actually——' his eyes were considering, assessing '—pleasure is just about the main reason for marriage. Always has been.'

The colour in her cheeks was her only admission that she had heard. She felt it flame, then die away just as quickly. 'I don't see how you could pretend life wouldn't be utterly different. You would, I presume, expect me to run your home, and I'm a rotten housewife.' The warning was offered defiantly, as if it was something she was determined upon.

'I don't believe that, not Friede's grand-daughter.' He was openly laughing at her now; she had to struggle against her inclination to share his amusement.

'Well...'

'In any case, that would be entirely up to you. I'm a rich man, Nicole, my wife can choose how she spends her time. If she wants to paint, there's no problem. I have my flat serviced, food is available at the end of a phone; that will continue whether or not I'm married. And I promise you'll find the flat more comfortable than your student accommodation.'

'I don't know why we're having this conversation.' He could be quite persuasive; there was a note of panic in her voice and she put her hands against her ears. 'There is just nothing to discuss. I have no intention of marrying, and...' she had been brought up to be reasonably polite and her next words were semi-automatic '...that's no reflection on you. I've no intention of marrying anyone for years and years. Not until I've made my way in my profession.'

'Mmm. Well... In the scheme of things that's bound to be too late to help your grandfather, but as you feel so strongly there's no more to be said.' He pulled his car keys from his pocket, tossed them up into the air and caught them before walking to the door. 'Anyway——' he smiled, showing no sign of disappointment, though there was a tightness about his mouth that could have meant...anything '—thanks for coming out with me this evening, Nicole; I enjoyed your company. See you around some time.'

'Yes, I suppose so.' Disconcerted that there was so little protest, she found it a great relief and at the same time a tremendous anticlimax. Probably a reaction to all the tensions of the last twenty-four hours...

'Goodnight, then.' He looked down at her, the merest trace of a smile remaining. 'I'll keep an eye open for you in about . . . oh, maybe ten years. I'm sure by then you'll be having your own exhibition at some prestigious gallery.'

'I'd like to think so, but I'm not . . .'

'Oh, I'm sure of it. Hard work and determination are bound to pay off. Goodnight.' He opened the door, but before he had time to walk through she spoke his name and he stopped, looking down with one eyebrow raised quizzically, assuring her that he had noticed her previous avoidance of it.

'Yes . . . Nicole?' Of course he would underline it.

'Grandfather? The company? Have you any idea what . . . ?' It was an effort to force the query to her lips, it was so humiliating.

'What do you want me to tell you?' His voice had grown perceptibly harder. 'Some fairy-story that will send you to sleep with a clear conscience and a smile on your face.' He barely acknowledged her shake of the head but went on remorselessly. 'Well, I'm too much of a realist for that. The harsh truth is that your grandfather's companies are finished. I'm sorry about it, but there's nothing I can do. König is about to be hammered.' The door closed behind him and she stood staring till she heard the sound of the engine firing, the crunch of wheels on the gravel.

Her fingers shook as she reached out and slipped the security bolts into position. And her mind was blank with shock as she turned, pulled herself up by the banisters and went to bed.

CHAPTER THREE

'You had a good time last night?' It was her grand-mother who asked the question, and that not until Nicole was on her second cup of coffee and had eaten her toast. Opa had obviously been dying with curiosity and more than a little anxiety, but it was easy to conclude that Gran had forbidden him to make any premature enquiry.

'Mmm.' She felt rotten; a single word from her could take the look of strain from both beloved faces, but... Carefully she put down her cup and her forced smile was meant to include both. 'Very nice. I didn't know Bradgate Hall, did you? It's a private club, very plush.'

'So...' Opa, having looked at her over his news-paper folded it and laid it beside his plate. 'He took you there, did he? I didn't even know he was a member. Someone must have died; I hear that's the only way you can get in. You...see him again, Nicky?'

'No.' She struggled to sound casual about it. 'He didn't suggest it.' Why, *why* couldn't she just tell them what had happened...?

'Well...' Any lightness that had been in Opa's manner evaporated as he pushed back his chair. 'I'd better get going, there's a lot to be done in the office today. I won't be back for lunch, Friede—remember I told you those people from the auditors are coming today...'

'If you want to bring them here, Walther,' his wife said as she followed him through to the hall, 'you know I can always fix them something to eat.'

'No, Friede,' his tone was brusque, 'they can go to the pub for a sandwich. I don't see why——' His voice broke off and Nicole was conscious of her grandmother's agitated whispers before he spoke again, rather testily and on an entirely different subject. 'All right, all right, Friede.' The front door was opened then another thought struck him. 'Oh, and if the agents ring tell them Friday. Before Friday is impossible to look at the shoe boxes.' The door closed firmly. Nicole looked up as her grandmother came into the room; she was looking despondent, maybe even depressed until she realised her granddaughter was watching her, and she made an effort to smile.

'Opa, he say goodbye to you, Nicole, he has things on his mind right now.' She went to the sink and began to rinse out dishes.

'That's all right, Gran.' Knowing that he had said no such thing, that he had entirely forgotten she was due to return to college this afternoon, she resisted her inclination to go and put a comforting arm around the old lady's shoulders. It would have been such a normal thing for her to do, but somehow, with things so very far from normal, it might make the atmosphere still more fraught. So she picked up the towel and began to dry.

'Nice morning.' She looked over the sunlit garden and over the adjoining fields.

'Yes, nice,' Oma agreed without really looking. 'You go back this afternoon, Nicky?'

'Yes. Just two more weeks till the summer break. It can't come quickly enough for me.' In fact she was dreading the end of term, when she would be expected to be back home permanently instead of just for odd days and weekends.

'Oh? I thought you liked.'

'I do like.' Nicole forced a light teasing note. 'In fact I love. And when I'm a world-famous artist you will love too.'

'Oh, Nicky.' The remonstrance and quick smile faded rather too quickly.

'What——' the words came to her lips without any definite intention on her part; in fact, she had made a conscious decision to avoid any enquiry '—what was that Grandfather said about agents?' She turned to stack cups and saucers in the wall cupboard. 'Thinking of going into the shoe trade, is he?'

There was a pause. 'Estate agents, he meant, Nicky.'

'Oh…thinking of going into the property market, then?'

'Not exactly.' For a longish time hot soapy water was splashed round the sink which was then dried with a damp cloth and the taps were rubbed till they shone. 'No, not exactly.' Carefully she dried her hands and folded the towel with meticulous care. 'We're getting older and we've been thinking…for some time we've been thinking, this house is too big for us. Two old people rattling about in a place this size, it's ridiculous, so…it seemed sensible to look for something smaller.'

'But, Gran,' it was a cry of pain, 'you and Grandfather love Rosenheim, you can't leave it. It'll break your hearts.'

'Nonsense. Hearts don't break so easy. So long as I have you and Opa, both well and happy, my heart will not be breaking, I assure you.'

'No?'

'No. *No*,' she repeated with more conviction. 'Most people when they reach our age want an easier life, something smaller so they have time for hobbies and——'

'Hobbies? This house is your hobby. And the garden, all your roses...' She crossed to the side window with its view of the extensive rose garden and herbaceous border which were her grandmother's pride and relaxation. 'Where would you go?' Her voice shook very slightly as the harsh facts began to demand recognition.

'Oh, we haven't decided.' Oma bustled about the large kitchen assembling mixing bowls and flour containers, obviously intent on keeping herself occupied. 'We have some details, on the desk in Opa's study if you want to have a look.'

'Yes, all right.' Despondently Nicole walked to the door, then, on a thought, turned. 'You're not making pancakes, are you, Gran?'

'Pancakes?' The old woman looked up with a smile. 'No.' She shook her head. 'Why should I be making pancakes?'

By no means reassured, Nicole crossed the hall and opened the door of the small den, dark with wood panelling and heavy leather. Opa's collection of old Prussian hunting prints on the walls did little to make the room cheerful, but she knew they were tied up with his childhood memories, reminders of how far he had come from the extreme poverty of his early life. And he was on the brink—Nicole allowed the tips of her fingers to rub for a moment against the wood of the antique desk—he was very near to losing everything.

She slumped on to a chair and reached for the small pile of brochures, identified by the logo of the largest estate agent in the district. Easily managed bungalow, bijou residence, deceptively spacious town house, crumbling cottage ripe for redevelopment...

No. She threw them away from her. *No.* There was a sting of tears behind her eyes and it took an act of will to drive them away. No. She couldn't bear to think of Oma and Opa leaving this large house with all its graciousness and style, leaving this and going to live in one of those tiny poky places. Where would they put all their furniture? All the things they had gathered with such pride over the years, the pieces which meant so much to them. They would hate it and she couldn't bear it for them.

A moment later she had run upstairs and, without fully knowing what she was doing and why, she found she was moving swiftly, methodically from wardrobe to bed with all the piles of immaculately ironed clothes, then reaching into the high cupboard for her bag. That packed, she tidied her room, shaking out the duvet and quickly dusting the furniture, conscience-stricken that she didn't always make time to do these simple tasks. Her grandmother loved looking after her, spoiled her, she knew that, but she needn't always have taken so much for granted.

'Gran?' She pushed open the kitchen door and went inside. 'I think I'll just be off now.'

'Nicky!' Surprise lit up the old woman's features as she paused in the act of rolling out some pastry;

she looked over the tall figure in her student's uniform of jeans and T-shirt. 'I thought you said this afternoon, that you would be here to share some lunch with me. And I wanted to give you something to take with you, a quiche and a cake...'

'Oh, Gran.' Determined to leave in a cheerful mood, Nicole dropped her case and walked over to give her a squeeze, to drop a kiss on the greying hair. 'You will try to keep feeding me up!'

'Well, you young girls, I'm sure you don't eat enough. But I thought you had no classes to-morrow, I——'

'Something slipped my mind, Gran. I've just re-membered I promised to go in and finish some-thing I was doing in the sculpture class. A nuisance, but I'd better go.' She held her grandmother close for a moment longer than usual, struggling against the pain in her chest that was demanding the relief of tears. 'See you soon.' And she rushed off with a cheery wave of her hand, a breezy tattoo on her car horn as she sped down the drive.

Her mind was certainly not on her driving as she threaded her nippy little sports car through the busy city traffic with detached expertise. And when she reached the student hostel she threw her things into her room and began to rummage in her bag for some change.

'Hi, Nicky.' Her friend and neighbour in the row of cubicles they called study bedrooms stood in the open doorway, then sauntered inside. 'You're back early, aren't you? Thought we wouldn't see you till tomorrow.'

'What?' Distractedly Nicky looked up. 'Oh, hello, Mandy. Yeah...something's come up. I don't suppose——' she waved a five-pound note '—I don't suppose you can change this.'

'Five pounds.' The other girl shook her head. 'No chance, I'm afraid. Doubt if anyone else can either; bit too late in the term for that.'

'Damn.' Nicole frowned. 'I must make a phone call as soon as I can.'

'I can lend you two ten-pence pieces, is that any good?'

'Great.' She sounded relieved and stood up, pushing back her mane of chestnut hair with one hand. 'The moment I've made my call I'll get some change and pay you back.'

'No rush. So long as I have it by the end of the week.' Mandy dug deep into her pocket and produced the two coins.

'Bless you. You saved my life. I've got ten pence of my own, so that should be . . .'

'Who's the guy?' Mandy produced an apple from the pocket of her long droopy cardigan and began to eat, crunching noisily.

'Guy?' She opened her handbag and began to riffle, wishing Mandy hadn't hit the nail so cleanly on the head. 'What makes you think there's a guy?'

'What else?' Mandy adopted her worldly-wise expression. 'I'm sure it isn't your grandmother. Oh,' a thought, none too pleasant judging from her expression, struck her, 'it isn't Justin Booth you're in such a hurry to——?'

'Justin?' In spite of her efforts, Nicole couldn't quite hide the colour that rushed into her cheeks. 'Why on earth should I want to contact him in a hurry?'

'Oh, I don't know. Only, if you were, then I could save you the trouble, for I've just left him over in the studio. And maybe because I thought you and our beloved tutor have had something quite heavy developing.'

'No, nothing like that. Besides, I don't as a rule get involved with married men.'

'The times I've heard that one.' Mandy took a sour view of life in general and Justin in particular.

'Anyway, as I said, it wasn't to ring Justin. Now, I must go, Mandy. I'll see you later and let you have the money back.' She ran downstairs to the hall where several pay phones were ranged along one wall and picked up a dog-eared directory.

Randell Corporation—a whole list of numbers to choose from and of course the first one she chose was the wrong one. The second female voice announced herself as the chairman's secretary.

'Please may I speak to Mr Adam Randell?'

'I'm sorry, the chairman isn't available today. If you explain what you want and give me your number I'll have him call as soon as possible.'

'I urgently have to speak to Mr Randell now.'

'As I said,' the genteel tones grew a little more gritty, 'he is not available and——'

'Can you tell me where I can contact him, please?' She tried to sound as forceful and determined as the other.

'I'm sorry.'

'Then please——' her courage was beginning to flag; if she didn't get on to him soon her entire resolve would slip away, and she might regret it for the rest of her life '—give me his home number, it really——'

'I couldn't possibly do that!' Shock, horror! 'It would be entirely unethical.'

With the utmost exercise of self-control Nicole stifled the word that came to her lips and banged down the receiver. Damn the woman. And damn him too. What made men so self-important that they had to have the protection of a female dragon?

Her finger was running down the list of names again. She turned a page, sighing in exasperation, then, as something caught her eye, she turned back and found it. She saw it, almost obliterated by the rubbing of many fingers. Randell, Adam, 10, Quiller Mansions. She was dialling the number, fingers shaking, assuring herself that he was unlikely to be at home and that if he wasn't then she would accept that it wasn't to be. Three times she had tried, after all, and——

'Hello. Randell here.' His tone was impatient and for a moment she was too shocked to reply. 'Hello?' Irritation was increasing.

'It's Nicole. Nicole Minter,' she added to jog his memory.

'Ah, Nicole.'

'Hello.' Her surprise at actually contacting him robbed her of any sensible reply; she hadn't even thought what she would say. 'You . . . you sound busy.'

'I'm on my way to Heathrow. You just caught me. I'm off to New York.'

'Oh.' Her spirits did a nosedive. 'Oh, are you? You didn't say.' Then she blushed. Why on earth should he have told her anything about his immediate plans?

'I didn't know till I went into the office this morning.' He paused. 'I don't want to rush you, but . . .'

'Adam, I was hoping to see you, but it doesn't matter.' What a very lucky break. Her spirits rose and she heard relief in her babbling voice. 'I'll see you some other time.' If she kept on like this her money would run out. 'It wasn't important, and I should hate to be responsible for your missing a flight. I expect——'

'I can spare half an hour,' he interrupted briskly. 'Where are you now?'

'I'm at college. Halls on the corner of Dagenham Place.'

'Wait there. I'll be with you in about ten minutes and you can tell me what it's all about. Nicole...'

'Yes?'

'There's nothing wrong, is there? Your grand-parents or...?'

'No, everything is all right.' Her voice was flat and hopeless.

'Fine. Wait right there.' And the line went dead. Nicole subsided on to a shabby chair and tried to control the shaking of her hands.

But by the time the long dark car drew up she was walking up and down on the pavement outside the halls, nibbling her finger and hoping he would be delayed so she could simply disappear. Just as she was deciding that his time was up, the car door was thrown open and she was invited to get inside.

She sat back against the cool leather, feeling angry and humiliated, and determined to ignore him. How dared he look as cool and detached while she...? Deliberately she moved away from his arm extended along the back of the seat. If she should relax she might brush against his hand; he might even—the very idea increased her heart-rate—he might slide his fingers through her hair and . . . She could feel those potent eyes on her profile . . .

'Well?' When he spoke it was mildly, as if his curiosity was aroused but only vaguely. 'You did want to say something, I imagine.'

'Mmm.' She looked towards the chauffeur, turned to him with unwitting appeal and shook her head.

'I see.' Adam leaned towards the driver. 'Stop at the Belmont Hotel, would you, Steve? It's almost on our route; we can have a cup of coffee before we go to the airport.'

'Very good, sir.' When they stopped the chauffeur got out and held open the door; they crossed the car park and went in to the large foyer. She heard him order coffee to be served at once and followed obediently while he led her into a small lounge, empty at that time of day.

'Now,' he nodded at the waiter who put down the tray on the table between them, then indicated that she should pour the coffee, 'you had something to say?'

'Sugar?' Crazy, that she was about to tell this man she wanted to marry him, yet she couldn't remember if he liked his coffee sweet. What had he taken last night? she asked herself in distraction.

'Nothing, thanks.' He took the cup, sipped, and leaned forward with a frown. 'Well?'

The colour struck her face; she had to force herself to look directly at him. The eyes were impassive as ever, at least . . . could one ever describe those unusual eyes, belonging by rights to a jungle cat, not to the human male—could one ever think of them as impassive? He was a hunter, she thought fearfully, and she his prey. His hair was damp, she noticed that inconsequentially; he must have been in the shower when she caught him. 'Last night,' the words were being dragged from her, 'when you suggested marriage, I——'

'I didn't know I suggested it,' he cut in abruptly. 'It was discussed. But go on.'

'When marriage was...discussed——' she glared but he gave no sign that he was intimidated '—I should have asked you ... begged you—I know you like Opa and Oma—please...can't you forget about the marriage thing and...?' A sob forced its way between her words and she paused, nibbling ferociously at her lower lip. 'It must be as unappealing to you as it is to me; couldn't you just help him financially? I *know* he would repay you, and——'

'No good, I'm afraid,' he broke in quite brusquely. 'You see, I'm not into philanthropy.'

'Oh.' Her mouth trembled as she fought to control her emotions. 'Well, in that case ... I realise there were one or two questions I ought to have put to you...' she could no longer bear to look at him '...before I rejected the idea so firmly.'

'So.' He drained his cup and put it down with a thump that had the sound of finality about it. 'Fire away.'

'I was wondering...quite simply...just...just what kind of marriage you had in mind.'

'Explain what you mean, Nicole. Happy, unhappy? Is that what you're asking? If so, then I confess that in common with most of my kind I have a preference for the happy sort. Or at least, in the absence of any kind of grand passion, for a reasonable degree of contentment.'

'You know that's not what I meant.' Her eyes flashed in fury.

'Ah.' His manner changed, became more reflective, assessing and at the same time cooler. 'You're talking of sex, is that it?'

She nodded once, her lips pressed together in distaste.

'Tell me, Nicole, how do *you* feel about sex? I think that's rather important.'

'I can take it or leave it.' It didn't in the least matter what impression she was giving. 'But at least when I take it I prefer to know and like my partner.'

For a second, anger, hot and searing, blazed in his eyes; sparks seemed to flash from them, so intimidating that she put a nervous hand to the collar of her blouse. But almost instantly he controlled his emotions, only the clenched teeth telling her that she hadn't imagined the reaction. 'So what you're saying is that if the sex side could be postponed till we get to know each other better, then the time might come when you reconsider.'

'*Might* come.' She snapped at him, unable to contemplate the future he seemed to be describing. 'And of course there would be my career...'

He ignored her last words, concentrating instead on the permanent restraints she appeared to be implying. 'Might come,' he repeated, then gave a bitter little laugh. 'You speak almost as if you hold all the aces, Nicole.'

'Wh...what do you mean?' The faint threat in his manner was unexpected; she knew instantly what he meant and experienced a sudden wave of fear... Here was she prepared to bargain, imagining she could dictate terms, while he... Was it possible that even now he might walk away from the whole project? She shivered, seeing all too clearly where that would leave her grandparents.

'I mean just what you suppose: that you are not exactly in a position where you can dictate terms. In fact, your situation is so weak that the slightest misjudgement on your part . . . Well, all I'm saying is, you'd be well advised to try to clinch the contract rather than impose conditions which might be unacceptable.'

'You mean . . .' Colour raced through her cheeks, and the hand that reached out for the coffee-cup was perceptibly shaking. Yet she would not allow him the satisfaction of lowered lashes, so she faced him with as much courage as she could muster. 'You mean, you would expect me to . . .' She swallowed noisily. 'To . . .'

'I didn't realise your generation was so coy,' he jeered, draining his cup and getting to his feet with an air of finality. 'But yes, I would expect you to——' He broke off sarcastically, then glanced at his watch with a show of impatience. 'Eventually,' he added as if suddenly taking pity on her. 'Oh, and to clear up that other matter: as far as your career goes you must feel free to continue your painting for as long as you find it beneficial, but one thing I would insist on . . .'

'Oh . . .' Her heart was beating feverishly as she stood up, waiting . . .

'I would insist you live in my flat in town.'

'I . . .' This wasn't fair, she hadn't gone that far along the path; her meeting with him today was just a means of clearing her conscience, and she would hate the reality of living in close proximity with this stranger. 'But I like living in hall with the other students.'

'Yes, I remember enjoying all that part of student life myself, but I must insist we give the impression of a normal married couple. At least as far as my friends are concerned.'

'But——' Anger, frustration swept over her again; she felt the jaws of the trap closing on her. 'Just what are you getting out of this arrangement? You can't tell me König is so important to you that——'

'I have my own reasons.' He looked at her icily. 'As you have. I am prepared to admit that capturing König is not the only reason, though it is the main one. Now,' again he looked at his watch, 'I must be off. Is it decided, or do you want some more time to consider?'

For a moment the temptation was almost too much for her; she was being offered an escape route but, intrusively, recollection of those grotty little houses flooded her mind. The misery and dejection on her grandparents' faces would forever haunt her if she didn't . . . She shook her head resolutely. 'No, my mind's made up.' She looked up at him, barely realising that her hand had gone out to touch his arm in a gesture of appeal. 'But, Adam, what if it's a total disaster, if we come to hate each other—what then?'

'That won't happen.' His manner had suddenly become more gentle. He leaned towards her and she felt the brush of his mouth, her nostrils filled with the astringent masculine scent of his cologne. 'I'm determined on it.' He smiled, almost tender, and she felt a rush of some bewildering emotion as she gazed back. Then, seeing his eyes move over her, she was reminded that she hadn't as much as glanced in a mirror since doing her teeth in the morning, and defensively she put a hand up to her disordered hair.

'I must look a mess.' Words instantly regretted; he was bound to imagine . . .

'You couldn't.' His fingers came out, circled her neck and gave her a little shake; there was something so casual yet so intimate in the gesture that her heart gave an unexpected somersault, her eyes fixed on his mouth. 'You couldn't look a mess if you worked at it. Now——' his manner changed abruptly, his hand under her elbow propelling her out and towards the car park where his limousine and chauffeur were waiting '—let me have a number where I can contact you.' He scribbled on a notepad which he slipped into the inside pocket of his jacket and stood there, totally dominating, blocking her view completely. 'You'll get a taxi back?' She nodded, inexplicably offended that he hadn't invited her to see him off at the airport.

But on the whole, she thought as she stood watching the dark maroon car turn out of the hotel entrance and edge its way back into the traffic, on the whole she was relieved. Glad that he was going abroad. Maybe now she could have a bit of peace and quiet in her life.

CHAPTER FOUR

THE last thing Nicole had expected was to hear from Adam again the very same day. And of course he would choose a time when the hall was like Piccadilly Circus.

'Phone call for you, Nick,' an anonymous male shouted, and thumped on the door of her room, just as she was beginning to immerse herself in a biography of Manet, a welcome distraction from her own more pressing concerns.

As she clattered down the bare wood staircase she tried to imagine who might be calling. She hoped it wasn't Justin. 'Hello?' She was slightly breathless, impatient now that she had decided it *was* most likely to be Justin. 'Hello?' she repeated more loudly, grinning at a bunch of her colleagues who were noisily debating which Italian restaurant gave best value for money. The line crackled briefly, then she heard Adam Randell loud and clear.

'Nicole? Adam.'

'Oh...' Immediate agitation. 'I...I hardly thought you'd be there by now.' She turned her back hunching over the receiver in an attempt at privacy, which was as likely here as at Hyde Park Corner, she decided in exasperation.

'I just got into my hotel. Listen, I had time to think on the flight and I've got an idea. I suppose you have your passport with you.'

'Ye-es.' Difficult to imagine where this was leading.

'Good. I've booked you a seat on a flight to Jamaica on Thursday—we can be married and——'

'Married?' She almost screamed the word, then, after a glance in the direction of the still arguing students, she turned her back and spoke with more moderation. 'Married, did you say? Surely there's not that much of a rush?'

'I've just heard something that says there is. The group I was telling you about are ready with takeover plans; unless we can thwart them right now, it might be too late.'

'I do have to finish the college term.' She hissed the words in a low voice. 'Or had you forgotten I am a student?'

'I hadn't forgotten. But I thought term was just about over.'

'It is, but——'

'What about Thursday? I understood things were pretty easy for you now, and——'

'There will still be ten days to go. I've no intention of missing all the parties and things before the end of term.'

'I'm not asking you to do that.' His voice was cold. 'There is a limit to the sacrifices you're prepared to make, I know, but you could be back in London by Monday.' There was a pause, then, 'Are you still there, Nicole?'

'Just,' she answered with what she hoped was crushing sarcasm.

'Well, listen, I can't get back from the States till next week some time, but I can snatch a few days at the weekend. We could meet up in Jamaica and get married there. I've been assured that it's possible; the only question is, can you make it? And will you?'

Nicole bit feverishly at her lower lip. Her inclination was to tell him to go to the devil, that she had changed her mind, that this was not at all what she had had in mind, she still needed time to get used to the idea—but ... Suppose, just suppose his very worst prognosis was in fact correct and her grandfather was in danger of losing everything. And—her brain was in turmoil, refused to function properly—he had said, implied, that initially it was to be a marriage in name only. Hadn't he? She could barely remember his exact words, but ... certainly she wouldn't contemplate anything else, only ... should she, *could* she ask him to ... ?

'Well, do you mean to give me an answer? I should have been chairing a meeting ten minutes ago.'

'All right.' It was almost a shout and held an echo of despair. 'All right, if that's what you want. You always get what you want, don't you?'

'Good girl.' He ignored the dramatics, was unmoved by the slight break in her voice. 'I'll have my secretary send you tickets and so on, and—oh, Nicole, I don't think we should say anything to anyone—I mean to *anyone*. Best if no one knows till it's a *fait accompli*, then there will be no chance of rumours flying about and doing any damage.'

'If that's what you want.' Her lips were stiff; she could barely force out the words.

'Well, goodbye. Someone will meet you at the airport even if I'm held up. Goodbye.'

And that must be a record in prosaic proposals! Numbly Nicole climbed back up the stairs, barely acknowledging greetings from the other students till, on the upper corridor, she bumped into Mandy and Rosie and promptly burst into tears.

'Hey, love.' Mandy put a comforting arm about her and escorted her, with Rosie trailing behind, into the haven of her own room. 'What's the matter? It's not like you to be down; you're the girl the rest of us envy like mad, remember?'

Nicole sniffed, reached for the box of tissues beside her bed and tried to smile. 'Yeah.' It was a joke among her group, a result of the gleaming MG sports car parked outside, that while she had been born with a silver spoon in her mouth the others were from desperately impoverished homes.

'Come on then, tell us what's up.' She plugged in Nicole's electric kettle and reached for the jar of Nescafé. 'Some man, I'd be prepared to bet.'

'What else?' With a superhuman effort Nicole pushed the tears away, tossing the sodden tissue roughly in the direction of the waste-paper basket. 'You should know that, Mandy.' She tried to smile but felt her effort was less than convincing. 'You'd be disappointed at anything else. If there's trouble, look for——'

'Trouble?' Mandy and Rosie spoke together, and Rosie continued, 'Nick, you don't mean you're...'

'No, of course not.' She frowned irritably. 'Besides, people don't call that being in trouble nowadays, do they?' In the normal way she would have laughed at the very suggestion, but in today's very much altered scenario her sense of humour had flown out of the window.

'Well, thank heaven for that, at least.' Mandy returned to her task and a moment later swung round with the mugs of coffee. 'There——' she settled herself comfortably cross-legged on the bed 'now you can tell us all about it.'

'Nothing much to tell.' Why, she asked herself in despair, why on earth did I allow that comment to slip out? Her only excuse was that she had still been in a mild state of shock and her normal discretion had let her down. She'd best remedy the situation as much as she could. 'It's all tied up with my grandfather and some business worries...'

'Oh. Just so long as it's not that creep, Justin. I was beginning to feel nervous again. I keep noticing those long, smouldering glances in your direction; same old approach, he uses it time and again. As I said, I've been worrying about you.'

'No danger.' Easy to say that now. In fact there had been a few weeks when she had been quite bowled over by their tutor, his constant attention, warm encouragement and easygoing personality producing an amalgam which was very hard to resist. And she hadn't. There had seemed little point and she had been on the verge of succumbing, of joyfully embarking on her first passionate affair, when the fact of his marriage had jerked her very firmly back to her senses. 'No danger,' she repeated with the air of convincing herself.

'Well,' Rosie, much the least talkative of the three, said, sounding less than convinced, 'we do know what he's like, remember.'

'Yes, I know.' She had heard of their friend who had left college and returned home in a state of depression when her affair with Justin had come to an end. 'Anyway, as I said, in this case he is entirely innocent.'

'Huh, if you believe that... Anyway, let's forget him. Tell us about this other man, the one who made you burst into tears a minute ago, and don't try to fob us off with that drivel about your grandfather, for I simply won't believe you. You're a dark horse, do you know that? I had no idea you were involved with anyone to that extent, did you, Rosie?'

Rosie shook her head and looked mournfully into her mug. 'Seems I'm the only person without man trouble.'

'I hope you're not complaining.' Mandy shook her head. 'Men and trouble go together.' She drained her mug, leaned forward to replace it on the table, then looked with determination at Nicole, who was wishing only that they would both go and let her work this out on her own. 'As Nicole seems to be finding out the hard way.'

'It's not like that, I told you.' Nicole summoned up a more convincing grin. 'Anyway, I'm not ready for any kind of commitment; there's too much I want to do first. What if I found I'd made a mistake, what would I do then?'

'Then you would join the club. My first time was a disastrous mistake,' Mandy reported with a certain gloomy satisfaction. 'But——' she grinned briefly '—I'm not sorry about it, on the whole. You'd probably feel the same when it was over. But then again, you——' she affected an expression of inane bliss '—might find it a divine experience.'

'You think so?' Rosie, apparently bored with the whole subject, got up, stretched, and took a step towards the door.

'Yeah, I do. But I tell you what might be worse even than a disaster. A total disappointment. A non-event.' She thought a moment or two longer, then came to a decision. 'Tell you what. To give you two the benefit of my experience . . . I'll sketch the perfect scenario.'

'*Mandy,*' Rosie was almost pleading, 'we were supposed to be going to Mario's to eat. My stomach is screaming out for food.'

'This will take just a minute. You would like some advice, wouldn't you, Nicole?'

'Oh, I can think things out for myself. I've got till the weekend, after all . . .' Damn, why had she said that?

'Aha, that's what this is all about? He's planning to whisk you off to his love-nest for the weekend and have his way with you and——'

'It's not like that at all.' The whole thing was out of control.

'Well, I'll say just one thing. Don't settle for a grotty bedsit in Brixham, will you, Nick? Insist on somewhere glamorous like . . . a château in France. I went to one once with Mum and Dad, a prezzy for my sixteenth birthday. Not too far from the channel ports—what was it now? Oh, yeah, the Château de Montreuil, that was it, I think. That——' the prospect seemed to afford particular pleasure and she lay back, hands folded at the back of her head '—is definitely where I would demand to be taken for a romantic weekend. Only——' a hint of realism began to intrude '—only I never seem to meet the kind of guy with that sort of money. Chance would be a fine thing.' Suddenly she yawned loudly and stretched. 'You feeling better, then, love?' She studied Nicole's face anxiously and smiled, apparently reassured. 'It always does you good to talk things through.' She seemed totally oblivious of who had done most of the talking. 'Come on, then, Rosie, if we want to eat spaghetti we'd better scarper.' They stood by the door, Mandy grinning cheekily. 'Sweet dreams. Maybe I should change my career plans and try for a job as an agony aunt. Give me a reference, would you?'

The door closed before Nicole had time to suggest that the question should be repeated in a week's time. And that was as well, she thought as she got up and moved restlessly about. She picked up the book she had been reading earlier and stared blindly at the page. Maybe talking, or, more accurately, listening to Mandy ought to have released some of her tensions, but she felt unsettled as ever.

One part of her, the sensible, down-to-earth part which was usually in control, was saying that she ought to go down to her car, drive home and tell them exactly how she was feeling—discuss with the most important people in her world just what she was planning, explain how the prospect appalled her.

But the other side, the vulnerable, uncertain Nicole Minter who was largely hidden from sight, knew exactly what their reaction would be. Whether or not it meant financial ruin for them, they would put her happiness first. When had they ever done anything else?

No. She lay down on her bed, eyes closed, a forearm across her face to shut out the light. She had reached her decision. All her life they had protected and cared for her; now it was her turn. She only hoped that what she was about to do, the step she was determined to take, wouldn't bring in its train more despair and unhappiness than mere financial ruin.

* * *

In the airport terminal building Nicole stood for a moment, feeling lost and desperately alone, yet trying to conceal from herself the relief she felt that Adam Randell wasn't there. She had expected to be overwhelmed and intimidated as the tall, dominating figure came striding across to meet her, taking the small case from her hand, summoning a porter with a snap of his fingers. But, before she had time to relax, a young man, of medium height and wonderfully handsome, perfect teeth dazzling against his dark brown skin, came up to her, his manner touched with the merest hint of diffidence. 'Miss Minter, is it not?'

'Yes,' she smiled. 'I'm Nicole Minter.'

'I thought you must be.' His brief appreciative glance made her wonder exactly how Adam had described her. 'I'm Alain Gregor, Mr Randell's representative in the Caribbean. He asked me to fly up to meet you. I have a car waiting.' He directed the porter just as masterfully as his employer would have done and in minutes they were sitting in the rear seat of an air-conditioned limousine which was threading its way through crowded, dusty streets. 'I'm to apologise, Mr Randell was unable to wait. He is having to alter a number of his arrangements so he could be with you this weekend but he will be here as soon as he can make it.'

'That's all right.' Nicole wondered if he could read the indifference in her voice, wondered how much he knew about Adam's immediate plans. Not a great deal, if he had obeyed his own dictum; he wouldn't want to risk the chance of even one of his most trusted employees guessing at his intentions. But then, almost at once, Alain turned to her again with a smile. 'Just a few documents for you to sign,

Miss Minter, if you can bear another short delay.'
And she felt her cheeks grow hot, almost more embarrassed than if her trip were one of sheer pleasure
and indulgence. But, did it matter what Alain
Gregor thought? What did it matter what anyone
thought?

'Here we are.' The car had slowed, turned in
through wide gates and headed down a drive enclosed by thick palms, tumbling cascades of
blossoms and tropical vegetation. They emerged
quite suddenly into the bright sunshine of the late
afternoon, dazzling against the white walls of the
villa.

Not too large, that much Nicole noticed before
they drove under a canopy of creepers which gave
shade to the entrance, nor as opulent as she'd half
expected. The door was immediately opened by a
tall, willowy black woman who smiled a welcome,
introducing herself as Delia. Her sand-coloured
cotton trousers and safari top would hardly have
been out of place in Menton; she was as stunning
as a photographic model.

Alain was driven away almost at once and Delia
led the way into a large bedroom, going forward
to twitch aside the gauzy curtains which covered an
entire wall. And there it was, surely the reason for
Adam's having chosen this house: the view of sky
and ocean, brilliant blue scattered with tiny islands,
densely green. It was breathtaking, spectacular; the
ground curved round at one side, the whole forest
seeming to tumble headlong into the sea. For a few
moments Nicole simply stood gazing, every fibre
of her artistic soul totally absorbed by the majestic
splendour, only turning when she realised Delia was
offering her a drink.

'Tea sounds just marvellous. Thank you.'

Delia invited Nicole to follow her to the kitchen. 'Have a look round, if you like. It's small, just two bedrooms, yours and Mr Adam's, each with its own bathroom. Large salon.' When she had filled the kettle she led the way through the living area, studying the visitor's face with candid interest. 'Beautiful, isn't it?'

'Gorgeous.' In spite of herself Nicole was impressed; she had expected something different, maybe a bit more showy. This room was almost stark in its restraint: pale leather settees and armchairs, smooth wood coffee-tables, a few oriental vases, a head in black marble, dominating, primitive, set in an alcove which drew the eye persistently.

She and Delia drank tea on the terrace, and ate tiny sandwiches and huge sugary cakes. Nicole listened with only half an ear; she found the land and seascape laid out before her almost hypnotising. She half absorbed the information that Delia had been trained as a teacher in the States, that she had resisted the idea of working in New York, determined to come back home to find a job.

'Thank you.' Nicole accepted the refilled teacup, shook her head at the suggestion of another cake and decided she ought to make some conversation. 'It's a pity, then, that you can't find a job.'

'But I did.' Delia smiled amiably. 'I'm sorry I've been deluging you with facts when you're jet lagged. Finish that tea, then go and sleep it off. No, I was saying,' she went on as she began to collect the plates and put them on a tray, 'if it hadn't been for Mr Adam I might have found things a lot worse. I met him in the States and told him what I was thinking of and he agreed to make himself responsible for starting up a small school here. It is mainly for children who have no parents, but if we have room we take in other children too. I teach them basic subjects and give the brighter ones special coaching. We work mornings only. Then in the afternoons I'm free to do my own thing.'

'Oh...' This was a new facet of the man she was about to marry. What was it he had said to her once? 'I'm not into philanthropy.' Was that it? And yet... Almost dizzily she got to her feet. 'That was a good idea of yours. I'll just have a quick shower and lie down for an hour. I... I don't suppose you know when Adam will be here.'

'No.' Delia pursed her lips. 'Hard to say really. You'll have time for a siesta, and if you want me I'll be in my flat. The number's on the pad by the telephone.'

The bathroom was as luxurious as anyone could wish for, all creamy veined marble and gilt fittings, with a deep tub which Nicole promised herself she would sample before she left, and piles of fluffy towels and an assortment of shampoos and skin unguents.

It was bliss to stand beneath the cool douche and feel the grime of travel and some of the tension float away from her. Back in the bedroom, a pale satin robe tied about her waist, she paused to look at herself in the floor-length mirror, pushing a hand through her long hair, pleased to see that its shape was unaffected by the constrictions of the cap she had worn in the shower. Although why—she turned away from her reflection with a toss of her shoulders—why she had thought it necessary to spend so much at the hair salon she could not explain; it wasn't as if...

The bed was inviting, more so because she had been unable to sleep since Adam's phone call. She lay down, bounced once or twice approvingly then with a deep sigh let her head fall back on to the pillow. If she turned a little she could just see the waves, densely white, breaking on the shore at the far side of the bay.

And Delia had said there was a flight of steps leading down to a private beach, a little jetty from which one could dive into deep crystal-clear water. It all sounded too good to be true. Maybe she was dreaming and would wake to find herself in some bedsit in Brixham. Closing her eyelids for a moment, she felt her lips curve into a smile as she remembered Mandy's warning. She sighed deeply then, turning, adjusted her shape more comfortably to the bed, and was almost instantly asleep.

When Adam came into her room she heard nothing; she lay totally still, undisturbed by the soft light from the overhead lamp which bathed her slender abandoned figure in a soft glow. And his face was totally impassive as he looked down, over the thin satin wrap barely covering her, the smooth skin of her legs from thigh to ankle, the elegant arch of her slender foot almost an invitation. He merely stood for a moment, motionless, then turned abruptly, switching off the light.

It was the sound of music that penetrated the veil of sleep, disturbing her. The eyelids fluttered open, then closed, as she lay in the dark. The unaccustomed warmth, the crash of waves breaking on the shore were vaguely puzzling, till she remembered and was wide awake. The music, sensuous, melancholy notes, vibrated against her nerves, and she stood, pulling tight the edges of her wrap and tying the belt more closely about her waist.

Barefoot, she walked to the door, opened it and stepped across the hall to stand in the half-open door of the salon. At first she thought he was asleep and, much as he had done, she walked forward softly, watching him for a curious moment before she realised that she in turn was being studied through eyes that were mere slits.

'Hi.' His hand went out to still the tape and at the same time he rose to his feet, stretching. 'Hi,' he said again, and she had the crazy idea that maybe he was finding the situation as awkward as she was. At the same time a throb at the base of her stomach forced her to admit, for the first time since that very first day at her grandparents' party, that she was aware of him physically. There was a treacherous weakness in her, possibly something to do with the lateness of the hour, their exotic location; maybe more to do with the little personal things, the sight of his hair newly washed and beginning to spring away from his scalp, the smell of the cologne he used, unfamiliar but in some strange way almost intimate, disturbing and astringent. She was struck motionless while her senses tried to cope with the unexpected assault, then she clenched her hands tightly against her sides, struggling for detachment.

'Hello.' She tried to smile but found she couldn't. All at once she was noting how exhausted he looked, his eyes burning with a fevered expression, deep-set and shadowy. There was even a weariness about the way he levered himself from his chair and got to his feet.

'Nicole.' His eyes travelled her length, from the top of her head, over the revealing folds of the loosely tied robe, and her fading blush deepened. 'How was the flight? OK?'

'Yes, thank you.' She was tongue-tied, sounding, though it was not how she felt, like a visiting child on her best behaviour.

'I'm sorry I wasn't able to be here to welcome you. I——'

'That's all right.' Now she sounded pert, and his expression told her he had noticed.

'I touched down early yesterday and hoped to see you, but when I knew your plane was delayed...'

'Think nothing of it.' Her voice, in spite of an attempt at calm self-possession, quivered slightly. 'I didn't mind.'

'No.' He looked at her consideringly before turning away with a faint sigh which troubled her. 'I don't suppose you did.' He crossed the room, and she heard the clink of ice and glasses before he spoke again. 'As I was saying, I had to make a trip to the far side of the island, and the discussions went on rather longer than I planned. Would you like something to drink?' He glanced at her over his shoulder.

'I would love a glass of Delia's special orange juice; it's in the fridge, I'll get it.' Glad of an excuse to escape, Nicole went through to the kitchen, irritated when she realised he had followed and was leaning against the door, a glass of whisky and soda in his hand. 'This is delicious.' She didn't look at him until she had drunk some of the fruit juice. 'The heat certainly makes you want to——'

'What about food—have you eaten?'

She frowned. 'To tell the truth, I can't remember. I seem to have lost all notion of time. I vaguely remember Delia coming into the bedroom with trays, so I suppose I must have eaten something.'

'What do you want to do, then? Should we go out to eat?'

'I don't, mind, only...' in fact she was still feeling so jet lagged she didn't want to think about having to go and dress '...what about you?' She looked at him over the rim of her glass, imagined an expression of relief on his face. Maybe even people like him suffered fatigue, just like the rest of mankind.

'I ate earlier, so I'm all right, though maybe I could manage a sandwich. Let's see...Delia usually leaves something...' He opened the fridge door and poked about inside. 'To be honest I'm feeling pretty flaked out, and with the wedding tomorrow at noon a good night's sleep would seem to be...'

'Tomorrow? At noon?' Sudden panic made her voice shrill and uneven. 'But why so much rush? I don't...I mean, I need time to...'

'Look, Nicole——' He crossed the floor; she heard his heels clip against the marble, and there was something threatening about the sound. 'You know exactly why you're here, so don't let's go over it all again; it's too late for that. Besides, I'm not in the mood for coping with your inhibitions right now. Tell me, did you sign those forms Alain had?'

'Yes.' She felt snubbed by his manner; her tone was crisp and cool. 'I was very obedient, did everything I was told; I went to all the offices even though I was out on my feet and——'

'Good. Then everything is in order and we'll be married at noon tomorrow. That I promise you.'

She bit hard on her lower lip, determined that he would not see her break down, but it was a moment before she was sufficiently controlled to answer with at least an appearance of calm. 'And I promise you I'll keep my...inhibitions very much under control, provided you spare me,' now she realised she was speaking through her teeth, 'your bullying tactics.'

'Good.' His grin was so sudden and so unexpected, that it was as if all at once he had found some humour in their situation. She was so surprised by it that she said nothing while he continued his investigation of the refrigerator. 'Now.' He was still smiling. 'Now that we've cleared that up, let's have something to eat.' He uncovered a piece of baked ham, some tomatoes and a dish of potato salad. 'Mmm. Delia is pretty reliable. Sit down.' He produced plates and cutlery, skilfully carved some slices of the mouth-watering pink meat, handed her plate across and a moment later had taken the seat opposite. Then he had steered the conversation away from the matter that was weighing so heavily on their minds, and to her surprise Nicole found herself unwinding a little, heard her voice speak quite calmly about the journey and even give an opinion of the painting which hung on the wall of her bedroom.

'Come on, then, time you were in bed.' He looked down at her almost tenderly. 'Sleep well, Nicole.' His hand came up and touched her cheek very briefly. 'And I promise you a surprise in the morning.'

For a little while after she had closed the door of the bedroom, Nicole stood looking out through the open window, listening to the crash of waves on the shore below, unconscious of the fact that her fingers were resting on the spot where his had been. She had this strange feeling inside which she had been trying to define, which she now identified as pain. Raw and naked. Then, when she got to bed, she was suddenly overwhelmed with misery and cried herself to sleep. With a silent desperation.

Oma. Opa. Nicole felt crushed by the need to have them with her today of all days. To feel Oma's arm about her, soothing her as she had done when she was a little girl, to feel Opa's hand on her head, patting her and calling her 'my girl' in that special way that made her feel so safe.

Barely aware of what she was about, she shrugged herself into a dress, sat in front of her dressing-table and applied make-up with a heavy hand. And there was a cruel satisfaction, almost a pain when she realised her lips were too red, the green eye-shadow too brilliant. And the dress, dark brown patterned with black, might look stunning on the beach, but in artificial light was simply drab and cheap. Just about perfect, in fact, for this wedding. She stalked into the living-room and stood in the doorway. Adam was standing with his back to the door.

'I'm ready.' Her voice was as cold as she could make it.

He turned towards her, stood for a moment, then was walking across with that imperious stride, lithe and graceful, past her and into her bedroom without a word. Speechless, she followed, not understanding till she saw him throw open the wardrobe door, riffle through the few things on the rail. 'You needn't.' A sob broke through the words. 'I'm not going to change this.' She threw out a hand to indicate her dress. 'What does it matter how I'm dressed?'

'To me it doesn't.' He spoke through clenched teeth, thrust a creamy dress at her and she shivered when she saw that his lips were drawn back in what was very nearly a snarl, thinning the normally pleasant mouth. 'But there are others to be considered, not just——'

'Others? What do you mean?'

'If you had been interested enough to pay attention to what I was saying yesterday evening, you might have heard me saying I had a little surprise for you.'

'Surprise?' She did remember. Vaguely, for her mind was still agitated and tortured. 'What do you——?'

'Your grandparents should be arriving at the Justice's about now.' He glanced at his watch. 'They flew in a few hours ago and I have arranged for them to be there to see you safely married. It seemed like a good idea at the time.' He strode to the door and paused, speaking with barely restrained fury. 'For myself I don't give a damn what you wear, but I suggest they might think that a bit odd.'

She stood staring at the closed door, then she wrenched at the offending dress and threw it into a corner. A moment later she twitched on the cream dress, an unworn memento of a holiday in the Greek Islands, mid-calf-length, of a crushed cotton material, gold edging the neckline and bracelet sleeves. Then with a cry she quickly cleansed her face, smeared on the lightest of make-up and without thinking sprayed herself liberally with

Gucci perfume before turning to the door, as ready as she ever would be to face the man she was to marry.

He looked at her, deeply, probingly, still showing no sign of approval, not even a nod or word. 'That's better,' would have gone some way towards wiping away the bitterness, but he just turned away. 'Let's go.'

But then in the foyer of the villa he paused, fiddled with a large shiny white box and turned round, holding in her direction a small posy of blush-pink rosebuds and a matching spray. 'I thought you might like these.'

'Thank you.' There was an enormous lump in her throat, and Nicole blinked wildly as she looked down into the cluster of delicate blossoms nestling in fern. She must not, *must* not cry. Feverishly she caught her lower lip between her teeth. If once she started she would never stop. And with Oma and Opa there waiting...

'Thank you,' she said again. To smile was painful, but she flicked a glance upwards. It was strange to feel so...shy almost; her anger was being dissipated in a surge of unexpected feelings which she couldn't spare time to consider. 'They're lovely. Where...?' She held up the narrow spray. 'Are they for the hair?'

'So I was told. Have you some hairpins?'

'Just some kirby-grips.'

'Then——' the topaz-flecked eyes might have been inviting her to share his amusement '—kirby-grips we'll have to use.'

Obediently she bent her head, felt his fingers brush against her skin while he fiddled with the hair-grips. It was a relief when he had finished and she could straighten up, surprised to see how bridal she looked with the half-hoop of roses just behind the crown of her head.

'Not quite straight, I think.' He frowned as he studied her reflection in the glass.

'But all right.' With a deft touch she made an adjustment and smiled faintly, disconcerted to notice in the instant before he turned away that he was wearing a matching rose in his buttonhole.

'I think it is quite the most romantic wedding ever.' Oma, her eyes brilliant with emotion, reached across the table set at the open window of the elegant clifftop restaurant and touched her grand-daughter's hand lovingly. 'We couldn't believe it when Adam rang yesterday and practically ordered us on to a plane with the promise of a surprise at this end.'

'Well, neither of us wanted a huge wedding, did we, darling?' Her new husband smiled at her, raising his glass in her direction in a personal and, she was sure, a mocking tribute. 'We thought this an ideal way to avoid a lot of fuss, especially as neither of us was in the mood to wait.'

Nicole felt a slow burn in her cheeks, smouldered briefly in his direction, then smiled with what she felt was sickening coyness.

'Anyway——' Opa flicked a crumb from the tablecloth, smiling broadly as he lay back in his chair. He sighed with complete satisfaction, an expression of warmth and relaxation on his face that Nicole realised with a stab of anguish she hadn't seen for many months. 'Anyway, you need not think you will avoid all the fuss. As soon as we can arrange, Rosenheim is going to have the biggest party. Oma will be baking and cooking for days, eh, Friede?'

'I dare say, Walther.' His wife shook her head reprovingly. 'But maybe we should allow the young people to decide. Truly, if they do not want a fuss... But,' this time it was to Adam she turned, 'but, Adam, I can't tell you how happy we are that Nicole has chosen to marry you. So happy. We could not have found anyone better if we had chosen ourselves. Only,' she warned with a charming smile, 'I don't want you to call me Grandmother or anything like that. Let it be Friede and Walther as it always has been.'

'I wouldn't think of calling you anything else.' As he spoke, he took her hand in his and raised it to his lips. 'You're much too young to be my grandmother.' Nicole, watching, felt a pang when she saw the expression on his face, gentle, almost tender like the tone of his voice. 'I only married Nicole—and she knows this——' he directed a brief smile towards his new wife '—she knows and understands that I married her only because Walther had got you first.'

'You wretch!' Friede König tried to pull her hand free but he wouldn't let her, and she smiled, confused, delighted.

'But, as I was saying, I'm happy with my bargain. More than happy. You know why, don't you?'

'Yes, we know,' Oma said cryptically, but before any explanation could be sought the next course arrived with a great flurry of waiters, and they watched while the whole roast sucking pig was dismembered and expeditiously dealt with.

Afterwards they drove with the older couple back to the hotel where they would spend the night before

flying off to New York at first light, something
Nicole gathered from the conversation that was tied
up with their business affairs.

'Show me the view, Walther.' Was it chance,
Nicole wondered as she saw Adam guide her
grandfather out on to the balcony, or was it a
deliberate plan to give her a few minutes' privacy
with Oma? She would hardly have thought he was
that sensitive. It was an opportunity she welcomed
but there was a touch of anxiety as well; she did
hope Gran would not become sentimental or she
would simply crumple and——

'Darlink, I am so happy. I could not believe I
would ever be as happy as this.' Her dangerously
tender expression had the converse effect of stiff-
ening Nicole's resolve.

'I'm glad, Gran.' Nicole put out her arms and
held her close, knowing that at this moment she
was telling the truth. She *was* glad, ungrudging that
her sacrifice, such a very small sacrifice, had freed
these dear people from the strains that had beset
them for so long.

'Only,' Oma sniffed and freed herself, blew her
nose and smiled, 'only, please don't think, Nicole,
that it's only because Adam is such a very rich man.
Opa and I think he is wonderful and we are pleased
for him too, happy that he is marrying such a
special——' she paused, put up a hand and touched
the girl's cheek '—such a very special person.'

'Gran!' Panic was in her voice. 'Don't . . . please,
please don't make me cry.'

'No.' Oma shook her head, laughing. 'You must
not; I refuse to be responsible for making you cry
on your wedding night. Only be happy, my dear,
and if you are, then I know you'll make Adam

happy as well.' She glanced over to where the two men were turning away from the balcony, and her voice softened still further as she looked at the tall young man. 'He has had such a *hard* life; he needs now to be happy.'

The words, so unexpected, drew Nicole's attention from her own feelings back to the man she had just married, but before she could ask the questions that were crowding her mind her eyes were caught and held by his searing glance.

CHAPTER FIVE

'So——' there was a coy note in Mandy's voice as she sneaked up behind Nicole and slid an arm about her waist '—going to tell Auntie how it went, then?'

'Auntie?' Deliberately Nicole misunderstood, though she couldn't quite control the warmth in her cheeks. 'What on earth do you mean, Mandy?' She returned her attention to her easel after a swift glance in the direction of the task her group was tackling: a wine carafe, a hunk of bread and an apple set against a draped length of material.

'Aha, she's blushing.' With her foot Mandy hooked a stool and squatted, legs sprawling in front of her. 'A tiny bit more shadow on the jug, I would say, love.' She narrowed her eyes experimentally.

'Think so?' Nicole considered, rubbed her brush on her palette and added a touch of smoky grey. 'Mmm, you're right, that is an improvement.'

'Well,' deliberately Mandy kept her voice low, 'are you going to tell me? Where did you disappear to so suddenly?'

'What? Look, Mandy, I don't want to talk here.' She looked warningly towards the middle-aged female tutor who was leafing through a pile of folders. 'You know what Madame is like; it's not as if Justin is taking us this afternoon.'

'OK. Shall we meet for coffee immediately after class? Then you can tell all.'

Tell all. Automatically Nicole continued dabbing at her work; this was her least favourite exercise.

She hated still life; how much she would have preferred working on the landscape she had begun just before... She sighed deeply, dissatisfied with her work, still more with her life. How could she possibly tell all to Mandy; how could she explain what had happened? Even if she could, it was unlikely that she would be believed, for how did one explain that in spite of having a wedding ring slipped on your finger sex had been the last thing on your mind? And even less on his.

Hard to explain that the man she had married hadn't offered even a chaste kiss on the cheek, just a quiet goodnight when they had got back to the villa. 'Goodnight, Nicole.' There had been a certain note in his voice which she wouldn't allow herself to think of as tenderness or even understanding, but on the other hand...

'Yes, goodnight.' Tears had been stinging again—relief, she had decided as she'd turned abruptly, forced herself to pause by the door. 'Oh, and...thank you, Adam.' She had spoken as if she were thanking a dentist for pulling her teeth. 'Thank you for arranging for the grandparents to be here. It was...kind of you.'

'That's all right. I always enjoy seeing them myself, and besides...' He had paused, and when he hadn't continued she had turned, seen him pulling down his tie, loosening his collar. 'Besides,' he had gone on in response to her questioning expression, 'I'm sure if we had...done it without them they would have been suspicious of our motives. As it is,' he'd continued to undo the buttons of his shirt as he spoke, 'I think we put on quite a convincing show. You didn't give the faintest hint of coercion; you're quite an actress, aren't you?'

His insulting approval had caught her on the raw, when she was feeling at her most vulnerable, and she had not been able to suppress the words that had sprung bitterly from her lips. 'Think nothing of it. I once thought of applying for RADA.'

He had raised an eyebrow. 'Really? Well, as I say, your performance deserves a nomination. Goodnight.'

'So!' Mandy was waiting when Nicole's class finished, kettle on the boil, mugs charged and waiting to be filled. 'Come on in, sit down and tell me. You *were* off on a wicked weekend, admit it. Where did he take you, somewhere terribly romantic?'

'Take me? He? You are determined a man is involved, aren't you?' Nicole sighed deeply, half inclined to deny the whole thing completely, but a demon of mischief made her long to study Mandy's reactions. So she sipped slowly from her cup, reminding herself of her decision to be extremely discreet where Mandy and confession were concerned. 'Would you believe, Jamaica?'

Mandy choked over her drink. 'Jamaica?' It was rather a good joke and she obediently laughed, but the smile faded as she continued to look at her friend. 'Jamaica?' she repeated with less scorn. 'For a weekend? You cannot be serious!'

'Yes, crazy, isn't it?'

'Crazy,' Mandy agreed. 'But I wouldn't mind having a slice of that kind of action. You're not having me on, are you, Nick?'

'I promise you not.'

'Wow!' The note of blatant envy in her voice had a warning effect on Nicole. She ought not to have... 'I don't suppose he has any friends who might be at a loose end over the holidays; I'd swop Jamaica for Torremolinos any day of the week.'

'You know you don't mean that, Mandy.'

'I mean it. I promise you I mean it. For a trip like that I would need very little persuasion. But tell me,' her manner became lighter, 'what was it like? Or maybe you didn't see a lot of the place.'

'Mmm, as a matter of fact,' it was a struggle to control her colour but she thought she just about managed to succeed, 'I ... we did get around quite a bit. Beautiful, of course. We swam a lot.' In spite of trying she couldn't blot from her mind that first sight of a lithe, dark-skinned body plunging from the private jetty into the sea; it disturbed her even to think of it ... 'And of course there were night-clubs; on the Saturday night there was limbo-dancing laid on. Fantastic; you can't imagine just how sinuous some of the dancers are, the women as much as the men, and——'

'And so to bed,' Mandy interrupted wickedly. 'That's what I'm waiting to hear about, Nick. Did it live up to your expectations?'

'Bed?' She concentrated her mind on that large king-sized piece of furniture, mentally slipped between soft cool cotton sheets, heard the insistent lap of waves on the shore. 'Yes.' She spoke with conviction. 'Bed was wonderful——'

'So, you *were* lucky.' Again that faint note of envy made Nicole regret that she had said so much; her relationship with her friends would be sure to change if they knew that ... 'Must have found an expert lover. What did you say his name was?'

'Adam——' Just in time she stemmed the other name. Not that Mandy was likely ever to have heard of the company, but it was best to be on the safe side.

'Adam,' Mandy repeated reflectively, then nodded her approval. 'Yes, I like it. And when did you and . . . Adam fly back home?'

'Oh, we didn't.' Then she did blush, fiercely, exploding before she had the chance to control it. 'He had to get back to the States. On business.'

'I see.' Mandy emptied her cup, leaned back on her bed and surveyed her friend suspiciously. 'This . . . Adam—he's not by any chance married, is he?' For such a liberated young woman Mandy had a broad streak of Puritanism in her make-up.

'Married? What on earth do you mean?' This was one question she had not foreseen and it was hard to think of an answer that didn't involve . . . Besides, they weren't married, not in any real sense . . .

'I wouldn't have thought it required a great deal of explanation.' Mandy rolled forward off her bed and stood up as if she too were regretting the exchange of confidences. 'But there you are,' she added dismally as if there was only one conclusion to be drawn.

'It's not what you think, Mandy.' There was no reason on earth why she should feel obliged to clear things up. 'I'm not . . .'

'No, I believe you, love.' The tone contradicted the words. 'Anyway, I'm glad it was good for you.'

'Oh, and Mandy——' this was something she had to get off her chest and it would be best coming directly from her, before Mandy got a hint from anyone in the bursar's office '—I...I won't be coming back into hall after the long vacation.'

'You're not?' Mandy was visibly shocked. 'What you're saying is, you're moving in with him, Nick.'

'I didn't say that, you know.' Now her face was flaming. With anger. She *was* angry that her selflessness, her sacrifice was being branded, diminished in this way. 'It's just that,' she shrugged, 'as I said, I'll be living out next term.'

'I see. Well, I'll miss you.' There was a short, disapproving silence before Mandy burst out, 'Have you thought how your grandparents will feel if they find out?'

'Yes!' Nicole yelled the word, then repeated it with more restraint. 'Yes, since you ask, I have done that. Quite a lot. In fact...' But if she let it slip that they were delighted that would only lead to more confusions and misunderstandings, and besides, she had had enough. More than enough. 'Now I've got some work I want to finish, so I think I'd better go.'

Quietly she walked out of the study bedroom and into the identical one next door where she threw herself on to her bed and allowed her anger, mainly directed at Adam Randell, though Mandy did not wholly escape, to simmer fiercely. What right had she to stand in judgement? Nicole knew for a fact that she had had at least three brief affairs, so how could she...? Of course she had this thing about all men being fair game until they were married, and she had decided Adam was married, and so he was, but... Damn the man. Even now she couldn't understand how she had allowed him to trap her in this very definite way.

Only.... she did know. Suspected, at least. She had suspected that very first morning of her married life when, waking early and supposing herself to be the only one out of bed, she had run lightly down the cliff path intent on discovering whether the ocean was as gorgeous as it looked.

It was then, just as she'd rushed round the last corner, as she'd turned away from the cliff, that she had seen Adam Randell propel himself forward, strike out into the cobalt water. And her heart had begun to beat in long, agitated strokes that took some explaining. She had been about to steal silently away when his powerful crawl had brought him round on a course parallel with the beach and he had caught sight of her, throwing back his head and raising a hand in greeting.

'Good morning, Nicole.' A few strokes brought him within speaking distance. He pushed the dripping hair from his face, and the sun seemed to catch each clinging drop and turn it to crystal. Her face was stiff with the effort to be casual.

'Good . . . good morning.'

'Come on in, the water's glorious.'

Only then did she make up her mind and walk forward. It would be fatal to allow him to guess at the reaction he was causing.

'You slept well?'

'Very well.' No need to elaborate. In fact she had fallen instantly into a sleep of sheer emotional exhaustion. 'You?'

'Me too. I was out on my feet. Are you coming in?' Still she appeared hesitant. 'We can swim out to that island before we go up for breakfast.'

There was nothing for it but to discard the beach wrap, to throw aside her protection, and while she did so she watched covertly through the thick fall of her hair. And although he looked he showed not the least sign of appreciation, not of the white ribbed swim-suit which clung to her like a second skin, nor of the narrow waist, the length of leg, nor of the very feminine outline. Damn the man. She paused, one foot deliberately extended, arched while she made a pretence of fiddling with a strap. But for all the reaction she got she might have been his grandmother. Which made it still more irritating that she did not, could not possibly look on him as if he were Opa.

At breakfast, served by a pleasant girl who showed not the slightest surprise at finding a strange woman on the terrace, Adam seemed slightly withdrawn, eyes hidden behind shades so it was difficult to guess at what he was thinking. And any conversation she tried to make seemed to die a natural death.

'What did you say?' he asked, jerking his head round from his intense study of a yacht tacking back and forth just below the horizon. 'I'm sorry, I was——'

'I just asked about Delia. I think she said she lives in the flat above the garage.' Her tone was deliberately crisp. 'Shall we see anything of her?'

'I doubt it.' He held out his cup for refilling. 'She teaches school, did she tell you that?' Her nod confirmed it. 'In fact, it's an arrangement that suits both of us. She has the run of the terrace when there's no one here, keeps an eye on the place generally, but she refuses to intrude when there's anyone in the house. As I say, it's handy for both of us.' His tone was very nearly morose, and after a little while he excused himself, asking her if she could amuse herself for an hour or two while he dealt with some business.

After that, Nicole didn't see him for the rest of the morning, though she did hear his voice from time to time. Presumably—she allowed the book she was reading to slip from her fingers as she lay on her sun-bed, drowsing in the shade—presumably he was making more world-shattering financial deals, grabbing still more of the world's limited resources for himself. Swallowing up small companies just as he had done with König. Tears came to her eyes; she pressed them tightly closed and stopped them spilling down her cheeks.

And she was awakened by the clinking of ice against glass. She looked up into a dazzling kaleidoscope of light and colour which in a moment cleared, allowing her to see Adam standing in front of her holding out a drink.

He was smiling as he sat down, his manner mild as if he regretted the prickliness that had sprung up between them. 'I thought we might have a look round the island this afternoon. There's a wonderful beach just a few miles away, quite isolated, if you can bear the thought of swimming again, that is.'

'Mmm.' Nicole sat up, sipped from the glass. 'This is delicious. What is it?'

'Totally innocuous.' He smiled, leaned across so his head was close to hers. 'You see, I'm getting to know how you feel, and I agree, there's too much reaching for the bottle these days. Simply fruit juice, lime, sugar, masses of ice and a spot of bitters. Not bad, is it?'

'Lovely.' She sipped. 'But this beach you mentioned——' She wasn't sure . . . there was something about the idea of being alone with him on some beach . . . it made her feel vulnerable. 'If it's so isolated, how do we get there?'

'By boat, didn't I say? I have a small launch and we can be there in fifteen minutes if you'd care to do that. But perhaps you would rather rest.'

'No.' Impossible to explain why she was so suddenly averse to that proposal. The idea of lying on her bed, tossing and turning, tormented by all kinds of unwelcome images . . . 'No, I wouldn't prefer to rest. I ought to see as much as I can. You're sure you can spare the time?' She hadn't meant to be sarcastic but that was how it came out, and that he noticed was clear in the sharp glance he gave as he swung round.

'Yes,' he said drily, 'I did say I could spend just a few hours here, but I've tied myself in knots clearing a couple of days in my schedule, so we might as well make the most of them. After all——' he raised his glass and drained it, looking at her unwinkingly over the rim '—it's not every day one gets married.'

And that, Nicole admitted with a faint smile when he had gone through to the kitchen to arrange for the lunch to be brought forward, gave him the last word.

The beach, when they arrived there, was straight out of a billion-dollar movie. A perfect sickle of pale sand, unsullied by foot of man or beast, fringed by palms leaning towards the heavenly blue of the ocean, offering abundant shade.

'There.' When he had beached the craft gently on the sloping sea-bed, Adam threw out an anchor and stood in the prow. 'There's where we usually camp.'

Repressing the inclination to ask who he meant by 'we'—it was none of her damned business after all—Nicole joined him, pretending to be unaffected by the length of powerful tanned legs in brief white shorts, the gleam of dark hair on the extended forearm.

'Come on.' He vaulted down into the shallow water and held out a hand. 'It's not too high.'

'I'm OK.' It pleased her to ignore his offer of help; she wasn't one of the helpless bimbos he was most likely used to. She turned to collect her share of the gear they would need and strolled ahead of him in the direction he had indicated, pausing while he threw down a couple of straw mats in the shade of the trees.

'It's utterly glorious here.' From the corner of her eye she saw that he was pulling his blue and white striped Breton shirt over his head, and she was surprised by the distinct tremble in the pit of her stomach.

'Mmm. My favourite spot to relax in the whole world.'

'I'm surprised.' She rolled on to her back, staring fixedly up through the dark canopy of leaves to the chequered shards of blue sky. 'If you feel like that about the place, why don't you just give up the rat-race? It must be idyllic to retire to a place like this.'

He grinned briefly in her direction, she saw without actually looking at him, then he subsided alongside her, hands linked beneath his head, feet crossed at the ankles. 'Yes, it's a question I sometimes ask myself, usually when I'm stuck in a traffic jam in the city or waiting at an airport for the weather to clear. Quite often at these times I ask myself what I'm doing and,' his voice grew more thoughtful, 'I've never given a satisfactory answer.'

'I've heard——' she yawned, covered her mouth with her hand briefly then went on '—or read in an article somewhere, that once people have a taste of power—oh, it can be in lots of different directions: politicians, chairmen of large companies, they are the obvious ones but it applies in the more humble spheres as well: classroom teachers, hospital matrons, trades union officials—wherever you have a situation where people jump to do what you want, then it's a very hard thing to relinquish.'

'Mmm.' He appeared to consider. 'That's your explanation, is it?' He rolled over to lie on his side so he could watch her, and it was impossible for Nicole to pretend even to herself that she didn't see him, impossible to maintain the calm, even tenor of her breathing, for one thing. 'You think I'm so drunk with power that if I eased out of business I would suffer the most agonising withdrawal symptoms?'

It was a moment or two before she realised he was teasing. 'I didn't mean that.' The moment she spoke she heard a snort that was a stifled laugh, and her response was as instant and uninhibited as if she were dealing with Clive or Jake or one of her college friends: she aimed a light kick in the direction of his legs.

And she found her foot unexpectedly trapped, was bewildered for a moment by her own reactions. Who would have thought that the rough kiss of hair against the tender skin of her instep could feel so...disturbing...exciting? And she looked up in dismay when his face loomed over her suddenly.

Half blinded by the sun, the contrast of light and shade, she stared up, was tempted to raise a hand and trail it down over the cheekbones, to touch her fingers to the smiling mouth. She was feeling vulnerable in a way that was entirely foreign to her, vulnerable and tender and slightly drunk. So unlike herself that, when his mouth came closer to hers, she didn't move away; in fact there was a distinct urge to arch her body a little closer to his, to encourage the brushing, teasing contact to deepen. But she was powerless, impotent, conscious only that the world had stopped. It was simple as that.

Only it didn't last. The kiss, if it could be so described, was over as soon as it had begun, and she had to blink feverishly to dispel the tears—not of disappointment; that would be too ridiculous—aggravation, more like. He had promised, hadn't he, that there was to be none of that kind of thing, and——?

'Poor Nicole.' His words broke into her chaotic thoughts, and she opened her eyes to see him looking at her, his expression enigmatic, not quite a smile. There was a twist to his lips which suggested . . . 'Poor Nicole, stuck here with a husband you hardly know when you would much rather be back in London with your friends. Am I right?'

'Not exactly.' It was less than a whisper. Not at all, a voice was shouting in her brain. 'I can imagine what most people would choose given the choice.'

'Not exactly.' He repeated her words rather ruefully, raised a self-mocking eyebrow, 'Well, that is something, I suppose.'

And quite abruptly he swung himself into a cross-legged sitting position, staring out to the horizon and sifting handfuls of sand between his fingers.

For a few moments there was silence, slightly fraught, then he glanced round suddenly, surprising her study of him, bringing scalding heat to her face. 'Tell me about yourself, Nicole. You wouldn't before,' he reminded her. 'Now might be the appropriate time, don't you think?'

'I'm sure you know most of what there is to know. My parents were married just three weeks before I was born.' Surprising that the bald facts could still hurt so much. 'My father gave in only under a great deal of pressure. I suspect he had to be paid before he would agree. You——' her voice quivered '—you can't begin to understand just how wounding it can be to know that your own father...'

'Yes.' His hand came out, took hers and gave a faint squeeze. 'I can understand very well. No one better. Believe me.'

'And then——' her hand was released; she had almost regained control '—my mother died soon after I was born. Imagine...she was just nineteen, and...' Again her voice shook.

'Yes.' His voice and manner were infinitely sorrowful. 'Life can be...difficult to understand.' There was a long moment of silence before he spoke again. 'And you never heard from your father again?'

'Oh, yes.' She spoke with determined brightness. 'Yes, I'm surprised my grandfather didn't say anything. Eighteen months ago, a letter came right out of the blue. He lives in America; he wanted me to go out and visit.'

'And...?'

'And——' she laughed briefly, without amusement '—and I considered it.' She shook her head in bewilderment at her own reactions, lay down suddenly and stared upwards. 'Can you imagine? I actually considered taking him up on the invitation to fly out there and have a wonderful holiday with him and Billie. His wife,' she threw in by way of explanation.

'Seems reasonable.' He spoke after a minute. 'You must have wondered about him often.'

'Very often,' she agreed drily. 'But can you imagine how the grandparents reacted? The man they saw as responsible for their daughter's death, now a threat to the next generation as well.'

'So in the end . . .'

'In the end I decided it was best not to go.' Such banal words to cover what had been so fraught and bitter. 'I wrote thanking him, saying I couldn't get away just then but leaving the door open just a crack. He sent me a gold chain for my eighteenth birthday; it must have eased his conscience for the years of neglect.' For a long moment she lay struggling with her emotions, grateful to Adam that he didn't rush in with words of comfort that would have been facile and conventional.

'Besides . . . I think it was for his own sake rather than mine that he . . . You see, it seems he's made rather a lot of money since he high-tailed it to the States, since he made his great break for freedom, but . . . he hasn't had any other children. Tell me——' her tone was brittle, and she threw him a painfully brilliant smile '——what does a millionaire do when he has no one to leave his money to? Cat and dog home, would you say?' She glared at him, associating him in her mind with the same ruthless class. Then she bit her lip and lay back with her eyes closed.

'That's a difficult one, Nicole.' He paused, then, when she didn't reply, he spoke again, gently with a hint of diffidence. 'And have you any regrets? About your decision not to see him, I mean?'

'Regrets? Why should I have regrets? He didn't give a damn if I lived or died all these years. Why should I feel anything?' She threw her thoughts at him with passion, but after a moment's silence she spoke more quietly. 'I suppose maybe a tiny regret. I would have liked to see what he was like, to judge for myself. Though,' she gave a faint laugh, shrugged to ease the tension, 'to be fair to the grandparents, they've never gone in for character assassination. In fact, once when I asked about him Gran said he must have had something, otherwise Liese, my mother,' her voice was unsteady, 'wouldn't have fallen so desperately in love with him.'

'That's true,' he agreed. 'I suppose, like your mother, he was young, felt trapped and couldn't see himself settling to the responsibilities of family life. Who knows, he might have spent years of his life regretting what happened. Heaven knows, most of us have plenty in our lives to regret.' He sighed, so deeply that for a moment she forgot they were discussing her problems and looked at him curiously, remembering what her grandmother had hinted at. And he was staring out to sea, eyes hidden, fixed on the horizon, his mind concentrated on something else entirely. But then, quite suddenly, he looked round and smiled, changing the subject abruptly. 'What about diving—ever done any?'

'Diving?' She frowned, shook her head, uncertain that she was even interested in finding out. 'No, I never have.'

'Come on, then.' He stood, held out his hand, and this time she accepted his help without even thinking of it, allowed herself to be pulled to her feet. And it was almost an anticlimax to find her hand dropped so readily when he bent to pick up his sunglasses. 'It's a pity to miss the opportunity when I have all the gear on board, only——' his eyes skimmed over her '—what about your hair; would it be utterly ruined?'

She smiled at that, a warm, relaxed sensation in the pit of her stomach that was very comforting. It was the first indication he had given that he noticed anything about her appearance, and she was touched. 'I think my hair might survive.' A moment later she had thrown off the cotton shift she had worn over her swim-suit, and was listening intently as Adam gave her instructions on the use of the equipment.

'You'll soon get the hang of it, but don't worry, I won't leave you. Sure you don't want a bathing hat? I just realised there's bound to be one or two in the cabin if you...'

'No.' She didn't want to hear anything about his guests on previous occasions, let alone wear one of their discards. 'No, I'd rather swim without a cap.'

'Ready, then?' He checked the buckles of her flippers. 'It shelves very steeply—that's one of the advantages of this spot, no need to take the boat out—so let's go.'

And Nicole found, rather to her surprise, that her first experience of diving wasn't the least bit frightening. She had always been a strong swimmer, and underwater like this it seemed effortless following where Adam led, skimming along the side of the reef, disturbing shoals of brilliantly coloured fish which darted away then, accepting them, darted back again, swimming in and out through their linked hands in an obscure game of their own devising.

'Well, what do you think?' He helped her back to the beach and bent again to release her feet from the flippers.

'Wonderful!' she gasped, pushing a hand through her dripping hair. 'The most exciting experience. All that refracted light, the colours—simply magic!' She smiled at him as he stood up, her smile fading a little when she noticed his strange expression. 'Thank you, Adam, for suggesting it.'

'Thank you, Nicole.' His tone was slightly sharp and its mockery was directed at herself, she imagined. 'It's always good to be able to show off in front of a pretty girl. Especially when she's your wife.'

Nicole felt her smile switch off completely, was aware of an ache in her chest. She bent to pick up her towel. It was almost as if her feelings were hurt. But when she looked at him again he was smiling, rubbing at his dripping hair as he studied her approvingly.

'You did well, you know that?'

'Did I?' These see-saw emotions were so juvenile—all for a casual compliment.

'You did.' Slowly he rubbed a hand across his chest. The faint rasp of hair was an electric current brushing her nerve-endings. He was studying her intently, must surely be aware of her increased breathing and . . .

'You're a very strong swimmer, aren't you? Surprising in someone who looks so very...decorative.'

'Christmas trees are decorative.' She spoke waspishly, intent on subduing the pleasure that was suffusing her now in giddy waves.

'Yes.' The golden eyes seemed determined to approve; she could hardly bear to look into them. Or away. 'So they are. So they are.'

And everything about him was so warm, so gentle that something very close to joy exploded inside her, threatening to blow her mind.

CHAPTER SIX

FUNNY how quickly you could fall into an entirely different way of life, Nicole mused as she poured coffee for her husband, watching him frown over some item he was reading in his financial paper. Here they were sitting at the breakfast-table like some old married couple, and yet their relationship seemed to have gone back rather than forward since the few days they'd spent in Jamaica.

Partly that was her own fault, she had the honesty to admit as much, for she had moved into the flat only after a tussle of wills. That had been four weeks ago, the moment term had ended, and her panicky request that she be allowed to go and spend a week or two with her grandparents had been firmly rejected.

'But they'll be missing me,' she'd wailed, using the tone that was so successful with Opa. 'They're used to having me with them from time to time.'

'I don't know about that. I should have thought they might be glad to have only themselves to think about.' His manner had been little short of cruel. 'After all, it seems they've had to devote about forty years to raising their family; in their place I'd be glad of a break.'

'You——'

'I advise you not to say it.' Now it was his turn to speak through his teeth. 'Anyway, it's not as if we haven't seen them; we did go up that first weekend I came back, and you know how much of a strain that was.'

Nicole had felt her face colour up. She had made rather a fuss about the sleeping arrangements, but she had been so nervous at the thought of being shut in a bedroom with him that ...

'Anyway, you're married now.' His anger hadn't abated. 'My wife, although I know how little the prospect pleases you, and I'm sure they'd be suspicious if you decided to go up and stay there. Naturally I wouldn't object to your going up for a day; I might even manage to go up there with you, and we could show them how blissfully happy we still are.' He had paused, contemplated her face for a few minutes, then got up, pushing back his chair with a screech. 'But perhaps even that wouldn't be such a good idea.' His tone had made her feel cheap, when it was simple self-defence that had made her fall into the habit of making her feelings unmistakably clear.

Nicole sighed deeply as she remembered all the sharp things she had said to him. Her nerves were rubbed raw, the result of the unnatural situation she had chosen for herself. And probably the most difficult thing to cope with was that he seemed oblivious of the tensions. Or at least of their reasons.

He had made no demands on her whatsoever. Apart from the one condition, she was living the life of a single woman, but that condition of appearing to be his wife was becoming intolerable. He was absurdly generous, had opened an account for her at his bank and told her to buy whatever she wanted, that the account would be topped up when the balance dropped below a certain figure, but he didn't even seem to notice when she bought something new.

One day, when she'd thought she had the flat to herself, she had washed her hair, emerged from her bedroom dressed in the skimpiest bra and panties and had bumped straight into him when he had walked out of the sitting-room.

'Hi.' He had grinned down at her as if she were a little girl. 'What are you up to? Washing your hair?'

'What do you think?' Her tone was scathing, rude almost; she was sick of his refusal to see her as an adult member of the opposite sex. Quite deliberately she ignored her inclination to run for the cover of her bedroom, and instead pushed past him and swung into the sitting-room in search of the magazine she had bought to read while she dried her hair. But she jumped when she realised that he had followed her, blocking her way, the expression on his face intimidating.

'You know——' his eyes were on her face, apparently oblivious of the swelling curves of her bosom now rising and falling in agitation, and there was a light of anger about him, as if he was having trouble keeping his emotions under control '—for a girl who has been educated at considerable expense, your manners could do with some attention, Nicole.'

She flushed deeply. 'Wh . . . what do you mean?' Though she knew perfectly well no explanation was called for.

'Just think about it, eh?' He turned away, picking up a pile of papers as he passed and subjecting her to a withering glance in the second before she heard the front door close with a note of finality.

She hadn't apologised, she couldn't bring herself to do that, but she knew his comment was more than justified. She had fallen into a trap when she'd answered him in that way, adopting a manner she would have used to no one else, and all because of some deep desire to get back at him. He was so invulnerable; she could keep her end up only by acting like some silly kid. Still...if her grandparents could have heard they would have been shocked. She would have been ashamed, she knew that, and she made up her mind to play the game with more subtlety.

The brief scene was quickly over, but after that she found herself watching him carefully, usually at breakfast, which was the time of day they inevitably met. Normally he would be out to dinner, entertaining business colleagues, and to be fair he didn't seem inclined to interfere with anything she wanted to do. Maybe that was why she found life so boring, time hanging so heavily. Most of her college friends had left London, Mandy and Rosie had gone back home, and that was why she spent so much time in galleries studying the Impressionists she loved so much, as well as any other exhibitions that were on. And it was while she was in the Royal Academy one day that she bumped into Justin Booth.

'Now, that was a piece of luck.' As they left he draped an arm about her shoulder as they walked. 'I couldn't think of a more satisfactory way of ending the day than to bump into my most gifted pupil.'

'Come on, now, Justin, don't lay on the soft soap; you know you have some brilliant people in your classes.'

'Isn't that exactly what I'm saying?'

No denying that there was something wonderfully appealing about him—the boyish insouciance, the laid-back attitude to life, even his faint air of neglect—Mandy insisted that was cultivated to appeal to the more soft-headed of his female pupils, but even that had an attraction of its own. Nicole couldn't help wondering about his wife. The shirt and jeans looked clean enough, but you'd think she'd take time to iron some of the creases out. He had bright blue eyes like a sailor, which crinkled up in frequent amusement, fair, curling hair, and a beard with a hint of ginger and a fleck or two of grey. Nicole quite saw why she had fallen so heavily for him in those first weeks of term, but she felt an overwhelming sense of relief that she had got over him so quickly. For she had, she realised with a sense of surprise; he was out of her system in a way that indicated he had never truly been in it.

'I've been on my own for the last three weeks.' You'd think he could see into her mind, was answering her query about the crumpled shirt . . . 'So I'm at a loose end. I was thinking . . . maybe we could meet one day and do some work together. If you've nothing better to do, that is . . .'

'That's a great idea. I've been having a lot of trouble with some perspectives; you could give me some advice . . .'

'I'd love to.' They had reached a spot where a busy main road crossed the park and they stood waiting for the chance to cross. 'You would be taking pity on a poor grass widower.'

She laughed at that, all the resentment she had felt for him washed away in amusement at the sheer gall of the man. She swung round to face him, didn't resist when both hands caught at her shoulders, pulling her close.

'You're such a fraud, Justin.'

'Don't tell anyone, will you?' After making arrangements to meet at the college, they parted, Nicole strolling along in the direction of the flat with a smile on her face. It was still there when she opened the door and leaned against it. What a philanderer. What a fool to be taken in by him. It just showed... Women ought to depend on themselves; were men ever to be trusted? Not by her, she decided; she intended to work hard, be independent and...

'You look very pleased with yourself.' The voice, cold and cutting, made her jump, eyes widening in alarm for a second until she realised Adam was standing in the doorway of his bedroom, drying his hands on a towel, staring at her with a most peculiar expression.

'Oh, hello, Adam. I didn't think you'd be back yet...'

'I'm aware of that.'

'You did say that you——'

'I know what I said.' There was contempt in his look; he turned away into his room and she followed, her sudden boiling fury taking her swiftly into the room which in the normal way she did her best to avoid. It was large, the single bed covered in a plain eau-de-Nil cover which matched the curtains and took up the main colour in the patterned carpet. On the wall above the bed hung a series of prints, nothing about them was the least feminine. Adam disappeared for a moment into the bathroom, then emerged, not looking at her, but reaching for the jacket which had been tossed on to a chair.

For some reason the fact that he refused her as much as a glance brought her simmering anger to boiling-point. A wave of self-pity added another dimension to her emotional state. It wasn't as if she hadn't been trying recently, and . . .

'Is something on your mind?' It was her voice, sharp and combative. He continued to adjust his red-striped tie for a few moments, but at last he spared her a cold glance through the smoked glass of his fitted wardrobes. 'Because, if so, then I'd rather you told me instead of flying into a mood or whatever.'

'I'm not "in a mood", as you put it. I left moods behind me with my teenage years, but——' he swung round and this time she quaked before the sheer fury in his eyes '——I do object to seeing my wife standing in the middle of Park Lane allowing herself to be pawed by a complete stranger.'

A wash of colour flooded her face, and with a knowing expression on his face, a raised eyebrow, a twist of his mouth, he turned away, reached into a drawer and brought out a clean handkerchief.

'It wasn't a stranger, and——'

'He was to me. I *hope* you know him.'

'*And*——' she refused to feel guilty about something that meant so very little '——he certainly wasn't pawing me.'

'No?' He swung round again, surveying her with that intense, judging stare. 'Well, I suppose it's all a matter of degree. In my book a man who touches a woman in that very intimate way and who——'

'There was nothing very intimate about it.' But even as she denied it she was remembering how

Justin's hands had slipped lower than her waist, had cradled her against him for just a split second and... 'At least,' now she was blustering in her guilty denials, 'nothing you couldn't see in Green Park any day of the week, or——'

'That——' he paused '—was exactly my point.'

'You...' She clenched her teeth over the word she would have liked to throw at him. She was hating this experience of being told off by him, especially when she knew that he had some right on his side. 'You really are a prig and a Puritan, you know that? There must be a word for people like you, reading into a light-hearted kiss something that isn't there.'

'Really?' He took a step towards her then, and before she knew what he was about he had his hands linked round her waist, pulling her against him so that all the hard planes of his body were held taut against her yielding flesh. Nicole's heart was hammering against her ribs in the most uncomfortable, exciting way possible, the breath drawn from her lungs as she looked up into that dominating, unforgiving expression. Then something altered subtly; the yellowish eyes blazed, then narrowed. 'Really?' he enquired again. 'Then, if it was so innocent, maybe you won't mind if I get some of the action.' Before she quite understood his intention his hands had slipped lower, binding her still more closely against him, and at the same instant his mouth covered hers.

But between the brief caress she and Justin had exchanged and this...this drugging, bewildering experience was a whole world of pleasure. She did not, could not resist the pressure that parted her lips, allowing him to explore and tantalise the soft inner recesses. Her heart was beating in strong, deafening strokes; she was caught in a nerve-shattering maelstrom as his hands moved still lower, hitching her against him so that only the tips of her toes reached the floor.

Her shirt had parted from her jeans and one hand travelled the length of her spine, warm and caressing, bewildering, erotic in the way it brushed the vertebrae and... A shudder ran through her, one that seemed to find a response in him when his hand moved round, searching for her breast, finding it, one finger brushing against the tender peak so she felt her senses spiralling out of control.

Deep down in her throat a moan began to take shape. She sought to release her imprisoned arms, not with any thought of freedom, rather an instinctive desire to draw closer still, to link her arms about his neck and...

But before she could do as much she found herself quite precipitately released—rejected rather than released. She stumbled against the bed-end and put out a hand to support herself.

'A light-hearted kiss?' In spite of the coolness of his tone she could see the swift rise and fall of his chest, and his face surely looked paler than usual. 'That was what you called it, wasn't it? Then you can have no possible reason for refusing to share one with the man you married. I won't use the word "husband".' He turned and his voice grew perceptibly more cynical. 'That implies a degree of intimacy that goes way beyond anything that exists between us.'

'That——' she felt so bruised it was difficult to speak calmly and in spite of her endeavours her voice shook '—that was our agreement.'

'Yes, of course it was. But I think I warned you that I expected you to behave like a wife, not like an available little slut from art college who——'

'I haven't met any of those.' She refused to allow him to malign her fellow students; they weren't *all* free and easy. 'But I dare say you have more experience in that way than I have.' Her gibe rather pleased her and it was aggravating to have it so completely ignored.

'And if I see any sign of anything like this in the future, Nicole, I can promise you a rude awakening.'

She was so furious with him that she was robbed of speech. In any case he was speaking again; she tried to clear her mind so she could take in what he was saying.

'So don't misunderstand me. I do mean what I say.' He paused, and when he spoke again it was with more moderation. 'I just came by to tell you I'll be away for a couple of days. I have to go to Rome to finalise some details. I did wonder if maybe you'd like to come along, but perhaps in the circumstances it would be best not. So,' he picked up a bag from the floor beside the bed, 'I'll see you in a day or two. You'll be all right?' He paused in the doorway.

'Perfectly.' She stalked past him, determined to hide the anger and, yes, she would admit it, the disappointment his words were causing. Rome. A few days in Rome. She could just imagine herself sitting on a stool by the Trevi fountain among the mish-mash of cosmopolitan students, all sketching away like mad. Rome...Italy... She struggled against the desire to burst into tears.

'Oh, and Nicole——' He stopped her just as she was about to leave the bedroom.

'Yes?' She held her chin high, eyes glittery and betraying.

'You know if you want to have your grandparents here you don't have to ask.'

'Yes, of course I know that.' Her voice was brittle. 'But, as you said a moment ago, we don't have the sort of marriage that could withstand close attention, so maybe it's best to leave things as they are.'

'You know——' maybe it was her imagination that suggested his tone had softened just a shade, and she had the feeling that his eyes showed some concern '—if you decide you want to change that aspect, you have only to say the word.'

'No, thank you.' There was a second of intense pleasure before she turned away from his darkened expression. 'I think I've sacrificed quite enough; I'm as content with the status quo as ever I'm likely to be.'

She leaned against the door of her bedroom and an instant later, when she heard the outer door of the flat close with a definite bang, she felt she had the freedom to throw herself on to the bed and give way to the pressure of tears building up so painfully in her chest.

And then, when the first paroxysm was over, she reached out for a box of tissues so she could wipe her face and blow her nose. For a long time she sat looking out of the window as the evening sky lightened and then was touched with a rosy glow.

If you decide you want to change that aspect, you have only to say the word.

And she, with all her stupid pride, her childish vulnerability, had rejected his offer with her brief dismissal. 'No, thank you.' When all she wanted, all it seemed she had ever wanted, was to feel his mouth against hers, his arms enfolding her, and then... But she dared not even contemplate what would happen then.

CHAPTER SEVEN

Two nights later Nicole was relaxing on the long, pale leather sofa in their sitting-room when she heard his key in the lock and a moment later the door banged shut. Suddenly the book she had been reading lost all its interest. Her heart was bounding in nervous agitation, and she got to her feet when he appeared in the doorway.

'Hi.' She was barefoot, dressed in a peasant skirt and blouse which had seemed appropriate on such a warm evening. 'Looks as if——' she shrugged, tried to smile '—you brought the Roman weather with you.' She was determined to be casual, difficult when all she could think of was their last encounter, the matter that had been on her mind with all its feverish and embarrassing consequences since he had left, the kiss which had been forced on her beginning to assume the most inflated importance in her mind. 'How was the flight?' she enquired brightly.

'Fine, thanks.' As he spoke he was making for his bedroom. The jacket which was meant for the hall chair slithered on to the floor and as she picked it up it seemed natural that she should take it into his bedroom and hang it away. 'But the heat in Rome——' he was pulling at his tie, undoing the buttons of his shirt and shrugging it from his shoulders '—was something else, really suffocating. All I want now is a shower and . . .'

'And what?' The muscles in his shoulders rippled, the chest, brown and silky, almost an invitation for her to touch, to slide her hands over the warm skin and... She wrenched at her thoughts, tearing them away from such an unproductive line. 'Would you like something to eat?' She stepped towards the open bathroom door then, seized with panic, began to retreat. 'I'm just going to...'

'You're what?' He emerged suddenly, dressed in nothing more than a brief towel which he held about his waist as he crossed to retrieve something from the case he had thrown on to the bed.

'I wondered...' She flicked a nervous tongue over her dry lips, all her determination to be unaffected by him disappearing through the open window, then, as he glanced up questioningly, she was able to continue. 'I haven't eaten, but I was going to make an omelette for myself, so...'

'Could you?' He looked pleased. 'I couldn't face a big meal, but I could do with something to eat. An omelette would be fine if it isn't too much trouble.'

As she bustled about the kitchen she felt almost mellow, certainly more content than she had been for some time. This was the kind of life she enjoyed, the simple, domestic things that brought with them a sense of intimacy. She didn't really fit into the kind of high-powered set which he inhabited. All this eating in the best restaurants could so quickly pall, and the beautiful kitchen—she looked round at the carefully chosen units in soft blue stained wood, smooth as satin—was barely used. Certainly it wasn't the focus of family life like the one at Rosenheim...

Don't get maudlin, she admonished as she whisked the eggs lightly and mixed a dressing for the salad. Your marriage and Oma's couldn't be more different. After a moment's consideration she set two place-mats at the table in the window; it wasn't a night for the dining-room and with the window slightly open they could feel a pleasant breeze off the river.

'That was really good.' Adam reached for the salad bowl and gathered together the last few shreds of Chinese leaves and radiccio. 'Amazing how tired you become of eating out.' She smiled when she heard him echo her own thoughts. 'What's this salad dressing? I really like it.'

'Just something simple.' And she was, too, simple to be so ridiculously pleased by his mild approval. She collected the plates and took them to the dish-washer. 'Would you——' she was half expecting a rejection and her offer was tentative '—would you like a slice of strüdel; it's——'

'Like Oma used to make.' He was teasing her. Her eyes opened wide in dismay; the merest *frisson* of pleasure ran down...

'Well, maybe not quite. I never did get the hang of all that pulling out; I bought a packet of filo and it's not bad.'

'I thought you swore you were the world's worst cook.' He ate a hearty slice of strüdel topped with a liberal dollop of cream and pushed his plate aside with a sigh of satisfaction.

'Well, now that classes have finished I got a bit bored the other day and...'

'Mmm. I have wondered. I imagine it does get a bit lonely for you here on your own so much.'

'Bored, I said.' She reached for the pack of coffee and the filter, measured four heaped spoonfuls. 'Not lonely. I was an only child, remember, I don't get lonely that often.'

'Yeah, of course.' He sounded pensive. 'I suppose that's *one* thing we have in common, though for different reasons.'

'Oh?' She raised an enquiring eyebrow as she filled the pot with boiling water, set out the coffee things on the table.

'Yes, I value my seclusion because I never had any as a child. Orphanages don't run to privacy much.'

'Oh!' She whirled round, feeling a stab of anguish that she hadn't known, hadn't troubled to ask about his childhood; almost all she knew was that he had no parents or relatives. And a stab of intense sympathy when she realised how fortunate she had been with her loving home and grand-parents. 'I didn't know...'

'Of course, you wouldn't. But it was nothing really; I never knew anything else and we were well looked after. I still go and visit one of the matrons. She was kind to all of us, a real motherly soul, and she encouraged all of us to get out there and do something. There's nothing——'

'But I would have thought——' She cut into what he was saying then stopped abruptly, pouring out the coffee with a show of intense concentration.

'Yes?' He leaned back in his chair and looked at her encouragingly. 'You would have thought... what?'

'I'd have thought... first, that you'd have had a fairly conventional education—you know, public school, then Oxford; you do seem to have that sort of veneer——'

'Well, you're right to a certain extent. I won a scholarship to a minor public school; I went there as a day boy and back to the home in the evenings and for holidays. That was tough at first, I had to put up with a bit of ribbing, mild bullying from both sides, but maybe in a way that acted as a spur—I got my head down and worked hard. In fact——' he grinned briefly '—you might say that has become a habit. Later, I got to Cambridge— sorry about Oxford—then a Harvard scholarship, went to the business school there, and that was how it all began.' He shrugged. 'Anyway, as I said, there's no reason to feel sorry for me. Certainly I'm not sorry for myself.' He picked up the coffee- cup which she had just refilled. 'Would you mind if I finish this in the other room? There are some papers I must look at.' And he had gone without waiting for her permission or approval.

No reason to feel sorry for him. She loaded the dishes into the machine. That was what he had said, but in spite of his words she did feel sorry, under- standing, even more than before, just how precious her relationship with her grandparents was, how small the sacrifice she was making. In fact she had ceased to think of it along those lines.

In the sitting-room he was relaxed in his favourite chair, frowning over his documents. The room had grown dim and he had switched on a lamp. For a moment she had the inclination to admonish him, to tell him he ought to relax more, that too much work could bring on... Then his hand reached out for a switch and soft, beguiling notes began to fill the room.

Nicole sighed. There was something vaguely sad and nostalgic about it. She picked up her book, kicked off the sandals again and tried to get back into the mainstream of the story.

'What's that piece of music?' When he got up and began to cross to the door she looked up at him.

'What?' He looked down, surprised to see her there judging by his expression. 'Oh, that's "Valse triste". Sibelius. Not really sad—pensive and in some way comforting, I've always thought.'

Nicole didn't reply, largely because he had disappeared into the hall. She heard him go into the kitchen with his cup, then to his bedroom, but mainly her mind was concentrated. She was trying to determine, was pretty well certain that he had played the very same piece of music their first evening in Jamaica. 'Valse triste'. How very, very appropriate. She felt a sudden burst of indignation that threatened the mellow hopefulness of the entire evening.

Angrily she flicked at a light switch and went back to her book, trying to flog her rapidly diminishing interest in the subject. Then, when Adam returned unexpectedly and sat down at the other end of the settee, she had to make an effort not to react like a scalded cat. And she refused to look up from her reading, though the words in front of her eyes were a mere blur, her pulse was racing and she was absurdly conscious of her bare foot almost reaching his thigh.

He was wearing a casual shirt checked in blue and white, cuffs folded back to show brown forearms, the scatter of dark silky hairs acting on her like a powerful stimulant.

Without any warning he stretched out a hand and caught her foot, circling the instep with cool strong fingers. Nicole gasped but forced herself to adopt a lazy, questioning demeanour totally at variance with her agitation. It was oh, so difficult to retain her composure when his face was shadowy, eyes hidden so she had no means of knowing... Experimentally she tried to ease her foot without allowing him to guess at her nervy vulnerability, but she was firmly caught, the pressure of his fingers, the slight but potent movement of his thumb against the tender skin of her instep very, very upsetting.

'I'm sorry you feel lonely, Nicole.' It was an age before he spoke, and then his tone was so low that she had to incline her head so she could hear the words.

'I wasn't. I told you.' It was infinitely risky to allow him to imagine... 'Bored, I said, not lonely. There is a difference.' Her own voice was soft, gentle, she hoped... maybe... would he see it as an invitation?

'Mmm.' He appeared to consider. 'Still... I told you, didn't I, that I was buying a place in the country? I think we should try and go down there some time, see if there's anything you'd want to change. It all looks pretty good to me, but I'm no expert; I'm hoping that with your eye for line and colour you'll be able to put your finger on possible improvements.'

'I've never done anything like that but... of course, if you want me to help you.'

'There is some work to be done, extra bathrooms to be put in, but I think you'll love it.'

'You make me curious.'

'Well, I'll try to make a free day soon, or a weekend; we could go down, stay the night, make a bit of a break.'

'Yes.' Her voice was weak and faraway, and she didn't know if she felt strong enough to face the strain. 'I'd like that.' She felt her foot released and at once began to get to her feet. The sooner she was in her room with the door closed, the better.

'Oh——' Adam produced a smartly wrapped package and tossed it on to the seat between them '—a present from Rome.' He rose and stretched, smiling down at her. 'Peace offering.'

'Oh . . .' Her blush must have told him she knew he was referring to the scene on the day he left. 'Thank you.' She pulled at the gold ribbon, slid a finger under the smart black and gold paper. 'What is it?' She smiled up at him, surprising a strange expression in his eyes, an expression that made her return her attention swiftly to the parcel.

'Oh, it's simply gorgeous!' She pulled the soft folds of the silk square over her fingers, admiring the kaleidoscope of muted pinks and greens; she held it against her skin and stepped close to a mirror to test the colours. 'Thank you, Adam.' She felt ridiculously shy as she turned to smile at him. 'I adore it.'

'Good.' He grinned. 'The colours do suit you, don't they?' As if to assure himself on that point, he took the square from her, not noticing that their fingers touched briefly. But she noticed, felt slightly giddy that she noticed so much, reacted to his nearness, to the mood which was making him so much more approachable than he had been recently. Her tension increased as he draped the scarf over her hair, binding it lightly under her chin, at the same time holding his head to one side while he contemplated the effect. 'Yes, I must be better than I thought—the colours look wonderful with your hair, Nicole. But then,' there was a mesmeric quality about him, so that she felt powerless to look anywhere else, 'I think all the credit is due to your hair, and none to Gucci.' He bent his head as she had been so powerfully willing him to do and touched his mouth to hers.

She gave a shuddering little sigh and began to relax against him, anticipating the joy and pleasure that was about to envelop her, but she had barely time to enjoy the sensation when he put his hands on her upper arms and held her away. 'I'm glad you like it.' His appreciative smile faded as he turned away, 'Well, if you'll excuse me I think I'll hit the sack. I'm out on my feet; I'll be asleep the moment I hit the pillow.'

But when she went into her own bedroom Nicole stood by the window for a long time. She felt lonelier, more empty than she had ever felt in her life before. And she knew quite positively, though she dared not try to put a finger on the reason, that for her sleep would be most elusive.

By next morning their moment of sympathy had faded. Adam was totally immersed in his business affairs, and Nicole was dispirited, disinclined to keep things going. In fact—she braced herself to a new resolution—life would be much less fraught if their relationship were detached. *And*, she reminded herself, she *was* planning to be a painter, and she had work to do.

That helped. All the hours she spent in the studio, the times Justin dropped in and tried to help. There was no messing about at all from him, just a lot of very sound advice which helped her trace one or two weaknesses in her technique. So when he suggested, rather tentatively, that she might like to model for him, it seemed only fair to make some kind of return. Besides, there was a lot to talk about; Justin was organising the autumn Rag Week which would take place towards the end of October and he was using her to sound out some ideas. So once again it was her tutor who proved the catalyst in her difference of opinion with Adam. Difference of opinion? That didn't even begin to describe the scene.

It was mid-afternoon when she got back from the studio, hot and sticky, in need of nothing so much as a cool shower. She grinned to herself when she remembered the T-shirt pushed to the bottom of her folder. She held it against her body for a moment, shaking her head in mild disapproval of Justin's bright idea, but then on impulse she threw off her clothes and pulled the thing over her head.

'Art College Rag Week' was emblazoned across her chest in huge letters while underneath, below a caricatured likeness of the principal and his deputy, in smaller print, 'Support St Ag's Children's Unit'. It was almost long enough to make a mini-dress. She spared herself another disapproving smile before she went into the bathroom and stepped under the shower, reaching for a bottle of her favourite shampoo as she turned on the spray.

My goodness! She stood in front of the mirror for a moment, staring at her dripping reflection. The material must be thinner than she'd thought, and there was no way... She looked ghastly; she reached for a towel to drape round her neck and tiptoed into her bedroom to find her hairdrier. There was no way she'd do this in public.

Possibly it was the hum of the motor that disguised the sound of the door opening, but a movement through the open door took her whirling round, and she sighed in relief when she saw Adam standing in the doorway. 'You gave me a fright! I didn't hear you.'

He didn't answer, just advanced a step or two into the room, frowning, his eyes moving from her face to the T-shirt plastered in the most revealing way from shoulder to thigh.

'What ... ?' He spoke slowly. 'You're washing your hair?'

'Yes.' They seemed to have been here before. She giggled in an attempt at self-possession but there was an underlying nerviness.

'And you usually wash your hair and clothes at the same time?' He was prepared to laugh with her, but then his eyes slid from her face and he frowned as he began to read the imprint on the shirt. 'Rag Week, is that it?'

'Yes.' She was relieved that he was taking it so mildly. 'Justin——' she hesitated; it was a name she should have avoided mentioning but maybe he wouldn't remember it '——he has this brilliant idea to raise money, a wet T-shirt competition, but ...'

'Justin.' His manner had changed; he was frowning in a way that dispelled any idea that he might have forgotten. 'Your ... tutor?'

'Yes, he's been a great help to me recently and——'

'So, you're seeing a lot of him, are you?'

'I ... I go to the studio from time to time, yes.' A hint of defiance invaded her voice and manner.

'Well.' He looked at her closely, deliberately, from the top of her damp hair to the tips of her toes, back again to rest coldly on her face. '*You* won't be going in for this wet T-shirt competition.'

Nicole gasped. It wasn't that she wanted to go in for the competition, she had more or less decided it wasn't for her, but she was damned if she would be dictated to by him.

'I shall make up my own mind on that.' He was turning away, so she followed him into the hall.

'OK.' When they reached the kitchen he turned round, his eyes dark with fury. 'I don't mind that at all. Make up your own mind and tell your friend...Justin, that you decline his invitation.'

'You,' she said, her voice shaking with the strength of her feelings, 'sound so utterly pompous.'

'Do I? You think your grandparents would be proud to see you displaying yourself like this?'

She felt the prick of tears. How could he bring up their names when it was he who had separated them, who insisted they stay apart. 'They won't know, will they? Or do you intend to tell them, to get them to throw their weight behind——?'

'I don't need anyone to throw their weight. I've said you're not taking part in this ridiculous competition and that's the end of it. You're not some Page Three girl, you're my wife and I won't have it.'

'But that is exactly what I'm not. I'm not your wife and never will be. Not really.' Now the tears were brimming and she was determined to have the last word. She whirled into her bedroom, was halfway to her bathroom when his fingers closed about her wrist.

'Don't,' he said through clenched teeth, 'don't count on that, Nicole. Especially don't count on it when you insist in parading about in that provocative way.' He threw her hand away with a gesture of contempt.

'I would have thought——' with the utmost effort she was able to grab a few seconds of control '—someone with your experience would be happy to help children, not deprive them.'

He raised an enquiring eyebrow, cool, detached, but said nothing.

'We're raising funds for the children's wing of St Agatha's. We hoped to raise ten thousand pounds, twice as much as last year, not that it will mean anything to someone as arrogant as you.' Then she made it to the safety of her own bathroom, banging the door loudly so he should be under no misunderstanding about the strength of her feelings.

She was lying on her bed an hour later when he knocked on her door. She was reading a magazine, at least trying to read; in fact her simmering anger had been a fairly effective intrusion. He opened the door when she called, stepping inside but making no move to come towards her. 'I'm sorry, Nicole, I have to go out.'

'So?' She spared him a single glance. 'What's new?' She flicked over a page but it was a mere pretence of interest; her heart was hammering, pounding against the bronze silk blouse she was wearing on top of pale trousers. At least he couldn't object to...

'Are you complaining?'

'Of course not,' she scoffed, throwing the magazine from her in sudden anger. 'This set-up suits me. I think the less we see of each other the better, don't you? It's the only way we can get along.'

'I don't think that's true. When we are together we don't make out too badly. Take the other night for example, when we met Gail and Peter Trent—we . . .'

'That night can scarcely be called normal. We were both making a great effort for the sake of your friends and——'

'I didn't find it that much of an effort. Anyway, don't you think that's fairly normal, that most married couples have to make an effort from time to time?'

She didn't answer, just levered herself up with one swift, graceful movement and went to stand at the window, staring down at the activity of the small square feeling moody and hopeless. Behind her she heard a sigh, was on the point of turning round in some small gesture of reconciliation when he spoke again.

'In any event, I thought I had expressed myself rather strongly about the man before; he——'

'I can't stop seeing Justin simply because you disapprove of him for some reason of your own. He's my college tutor. I can't go to the principal and say, "Please, my husband doesn't trust me, can you switch me to Mr Sandeman?" He, in case you're wondering, is just on the wrong side of ninety, with no hair, and he has trouble with his false teeth. They keep dropping down.' She quelled a sudden impulse to giggle, but the expression on his face warned against it. 'But he was in his day a gifted landscapist, and——'

'I've told you what I think, Nicole.' He spoke as if it was his final word on the subject, like some

Victorian patriarch who expected no questioning of his pronouncements. 'I'd better get off now.'

But she had one or two things she still wanted to get off her chest, and she would not be shut up so easily. She struggled against passionate accusation, which was her inclination, adopting instead a semi-interested, almost condescending tone. 'I still can't understand, Adam——' she moved a few steps so she was directly impeding his exit; her hands were on her hips and she smiled faintly '—just what advantages you find in this so-called marriage. I still can't accept that it was to get your hands on König.'

'No?' His eyes had narrowed to mere slits; in spite of everything she felt a cold shiver run down her spine. 'What else?'

Something in his voice, some indication of his meaning brought a wave of hot colour to her cheeks, and rather nervously she put her hand to her collar. 'I'm only saying...the benefits remain obscure.'

'What do you want me to tell you, Nicole?' Rather deliberately he replaced the briefcase which he had picked up a moment before. She almost backed off a step but forced herself to stand her ground.

'Just...' she shrugged '...it seems so strange, you don't get married till——'

'You're determined to poke and pry aren't you, Nicole? Has it ever occurred to you that maybe it's for your sake that I wasn't prepared to tell you the whole truth about that.' Looking into his face, drained of colour and taut with emotion, Nicole would have given anything to withdraw her probing enquiries; she didn't really want to know, it was none of her business after all, and——

'All right,' he continued in a voice that was harsh and flat, not like his own voice at all, as if he was finding some relief in taunting and wounding. 'You will have the truth, so here it is. Ten years ago I was madly in love with someone; all I wanted from life was that she should marry me, but she wouldn't. She went off and married someone else, a man a great deal older than me and a great deal richer. I have never been able to get her out of my mind or out of my heart, though I haven't seen her since we split up. I heard, through a mutual friend, that she was coming back to London to live, and because my feelings for her are still intense I didn't trust myself not to go running if she crooked her little finger. Have I shocked you, Nicole?' His brief baring of teeth could in no way be described as a smile, and she felt a clutch of pity in the depths of her stomach. 'So, that was one of the reasons our marriage appealed, though König companies had quite an influence as well. I wanted a wife, preferably young and decorative——' he inclined his head with a trace of sarcasm '—as a protection against my own foolish impulses. I'm old enough to be able to exercise self-control, as you hinted at the beginning of this conversation, but I would hate to act like a man in his dotage and grovel over what was refused ten years ago. There.' Wearily he bent to pick up his case again. 'That's just the bare bones of the story; it has its sordid side, but I'll spare you that for the moment. I hope it makes you feel better now that you know the real reason for our marriage.'

A few moments later Nicole heard the outside door close. But she stood without moving for a long time.

CHAPTER EIGHT

FOR the following few days Nicole treated Adam with a great degree of circumspection, ashamed in a peculiar way that she had provoked him into baring to her what surely must be both painful and deeply personal. At the same time her instinct was to soothe, to try to ease things for him, and the only way she could was by making their home life more pleasant. Deep down she felt hurt for him and absurdly indignant that any women should cast such a man aside for someone else, no matter how rich he might be. She was aware of no inconsistency in this attitude.

Adam too appeared to be aware that they had reached a crisis point, and he responded to her changed attitude with a slight lessening in his reserve. One evening they had been asked out to dinner with some friends of Adam's and she was surprised to find how easy it all was; she was very close to enjoying herself.

On the journey home in the taxi, she turned to him without thinking. 'Oh, I forgot to say, what do you think? The college has had a huge donation for its Rag Week. An anonymous gift.'

'Really?' In the darkness pierced by passing headlights his eyes studied her closely. 'How did you hear?' he asked after a pause.

'I . . .' She realised he was asking if she had been in contact with Justin and felt herself blush. Tears of vexation filled her eyes. 'Not how you think,

Adam.' Her tone was soft, very nearly compliant. 'I met Madame Thibault the other day, in M&S, it was, and she told me.'

'Oh, I see.' She saw the white teeth gleam in her direction. 'So the children of St Ag's should be all right.'

'Yes.' She spoke very softly. 'Thank you, Adam.'

'What was that?'

'Oh, I was just agreeing with you.' She turned away, smiling to herself, her suspicions as to the source of the gift confirmed in her mind.

Pouring out the coffee next morning, Nicole glanced across at him and felt a sharp blow in the region of her solar plexus. In spite of all the trappings of success, the immaculate business suits, the chauffeur-driven cars, the country house which they were planning to visit soon, she was sometimes aware of a vulnerability about the man, and she sensed that he could be easily hurt.

Surreptitiously she studied him, ready to flick down concealing lashes if he should happen to glance in her direction, which—her pulses quickened at the thought—which he did increasingly. But right now he was busy with the *Financial Times*, frowning over some details in a dull-looking article. Perversely she wanted to attract his attention to herself. 'Coffee?' She spoke without thinking, her hand on the handle of the pot.

'What?' He looked up, and slowly the frown eased from his forehead, his lips, while not exactly smiling, looking friendly. 'Oh, yes.' He raised his cup and drained it. 'I have time for another cup before I go.' He rose, reached for the dark jacket he had slung on the back of his chair and slid his arms into the sleeves. 'What are you planning to do today while I'm in Hamburg?'

'Oh.' Silly to feel disappointed. 'I forgot you said you were going there.'

'You could come if you like. I'll be busy, but you could spend your time looking round the shops. And I believe they have some first-class galleries.'

'Do you mean it?' She had half pushed back her chair, eyes glowing in anticipation.

'If you get a move on.' He stood drinking his coffee, then turned, 'That sounds like the post.' He disappeared and came back with a bundle of letters which he threw down on the table. 'Tell you what, if you feel like it we could stay the night; there might be a show you would like to see. We could have a meal there and fly back tomorrow some time.'

'I'll go and get ready.' Hurriedly she began to collect the dirty dishes and pile them on the tray while he leafed through the envelopes.

'A postcard for you.' He handed over a view of Fuengirola, then, just as she was hastily reading that Mandy was having a wonderful holiday and that she had fallen in with the most fabulous group of American students, he spoke again, the question in his voice drawing her attention to the large creamy envelope in his hand. 'Another one for you. Looks exciting. You're not expecting a legacy from any long-lost relatives, are you, Nicole?'

She shook her head, totally unaware of the shock and trauma that was about to unfold.

'Well, Hetherington, Binks and Meredith, Solicitors certainly have something to say to you.' He weighed the bulky package before handing it to her. 'Ms Nicole Minter, of 10, Quiller Mansions; another one who doesn't know your married name.'

Puzzled, Nicole looked down at the heavy cream paper embossed with the name of a Barnes firm. She couldn't imagine what they would want with her... Quickly she slit the envelope, pulled out a sheaf of official-looking papers, but all that was necessary was for her to read the covering letter. She collapsed on to her chair, put a hand to her face, but it was impossible for her to stifle the cry of concern that brought Adam's attention back to her face from his own correspondence.

"...to inform you that Mrs Cecilia Booth of Westlyn, Bridge Road, Lower Hillsleigh has instituted divorce proceedings and that she is citing you, Ms Nicole Minter, in her action..."

She was going to be sick, she knew she was, and if only she could reach her bathroom in time, if she could have a moment's privacy...

'Nicole...' She pushed Adam aside when he stood up and tried to stop her, reaching the bathroom just in time to start retching over the basin without actually vomiting.

'Nicole.' He was standing there beside her when she looked up, her eyes red-rimmed, stomach still churning with nausea. His voice, she noted, was barely a degree warmer than arctic, which was scarcely surprising, since he was holding the damning letter in his hand. 'Are you all right?' He offered a damp facecloth and towel.

'Yes.' It was a mere croak, her throat ached with the violence of retching, but she wiped her eyes and straightened up. Hardly aware of what she was doing, she led the way back to the kitchen. 'Hadn't you better get on...' All idea of going with him was forgotten. 'Your flight...'

'Have you anything to say about this, Nicole?' He waved the legal document in front of her face before tossing it on to the table with an expression of distaste.

'Say? What do you expect me to *say*, for Pete's sake?' It was an effort to push away the tears; a weeping wife might be even less appealing than an unfaithful one, especially this early in the morning. 'What *can* I say? It's just so——'

'Well, you might say if there is any truth in the charge. Has this——' he picked up the letter again and read 'has this Mrs Cecilia Booth any grounds for her accusations; has——?'

'Of course she hasn't.' The question was such an insult that she snarled her denial. 'She hasn't,' she repeated when she saw his impassive expression. She hiccuped suddenly, put a hand over her mouth as she wondered if she might have to dash to the bathroom again, but she looked up when he spoke, this time in an entirely different voice. Blank and almost . . . stunned.

'You're not . . . Nicole, you're not pregnant by any chance?'

'Pregnant?' She frowned up at him, as if the word were new to her and not fully comprehensible. 'Pregnant?' How on earth, she wondered, how could I possibly . . . ? Then in a sudden flash she understood exactly what he meant, and she was swept by such blinding fury and resentment that for half a second she was tempted to procrastinate, solely as a means of getting back at him. Only her pride, that stupid pride, wouldn't allow it. 'No.' Her heart was encased in thermal ice. 'I'm not pregnant.'

'Well...' He shrugged but with no suggestion of apology. 'You were trying to be sick just now. It could have been...'

'I don't have much experience of pregnant women, but maybe you have.' It was an idiotic remark, but even so his response was intimidating.

'What the *hell* do you mean by that?' If it was possible to shout through clenched teeth, that was what he did.

'Well, have you?' She almost subdued a nervous tremor.

'I do know,' he almost spat the words, 'that pregnant women sometimes suffer from morning sickness. I thought most people realised as much, but it isn't something that need concern us at this moment. I accept your assurance that you're not pregnant. Have you anything else you would like to say on this matter?' He tossed the letter aside with an expression of disgust.

'Yes.' Now that she was getting her wind back and the shock was wearing off, anger and indignation surged forth in equal ratio. 'You bet I have something to say! The whole thing is utterly without foundation and——'

'I suppose,' he cut in cruelly, 'This Mr Booth, whose wife is in the throes of ridding herself of him, is your...tutor from college.'

'You know that damned well. That is exactly what he is. My...tutor. I'll repeat that for you. My...tutor.' Deliberately she mocked the hesitation in his voice. 'And that is all he is.'

'Not quite all, I think. You realise now how foolish your behaviour has been. It seems quite clear that I wasn't the only one to see you together and draw what seemed to be the obvious conclusions.'

'A friend, as well.' Now she was very nearly crying. With frustration and aggravation. 'I've always thought of him as a friend...'

'You realise, if his wife is keen to be rid of him, that you've made it easy for her. You're sure there's nothing else?'

'Of course I'm sure. There was nothing else, nothing to tell, nothing for anyone to see...'

'Think. I know you've been meeting him. Where? When? Who else was there?'

'I haven't seen that much of him. Just when we've been working in the studio together.'

'Alone?'

She bit her lip. 'Occasionally. Sometimes I would be there when he came. Once or twice one of the other students appeared.'

'This studio, it's in the college?'

'Yes.'

'So there's no place there he can live. Or sleep?'

'He doesn't *live* there. As far as I know he lives in his house at Hillsleigh and——' She broke off, she was remembering that once or twice it had occurred to her that he might have slept there. The couch gave the impression of having been remade, and something else, just a vague idea...

'You're having second thoughts?'

'No, not really.' But her manner said otherwise. 'I don't know if he slept there. I suppose he might have, but he never slept there with me, if that's what you're getting at.'

'Nor anywhere else?'

'No, nor anywhere else!' she cried passionately. 'I told you, we were friends, that's all. I don't understand why his wife should have got the idea that I——'

'If his wife is anxious to be free she won't worry too much about that; she'll be prepared to use any evidence she can put her hands on. Anyway, I'll have to get on to this right away.' His face revealed how much taste he had for the task ahead. 'So long as I have your assurance that there's not a word of truth in it, and if no one saw you together at the studio I don't think we need...' He looked up when he heard her utter a sound, saw her fingers pressed to her eyes. 'Well?'

'There was someone.' She just remembered. 'Justin had been making a few sketches of me.' She couldn't bring herself to look at his face. 'Someone came to the door, looking for a woman we had never heard of.' She recalled the man's friendly, knowing grin and realised just how easily that could have hidden the real reason for his visit.

'I see.' His expression as he gathered up the papers and put them into a folder was stony. 'Well, as I said, I'll get on to this without delay.'

'There's nothing in it, you know.' She felt a quite desperate need to justify herself. 'Not a shred of evidence and not a word of truth.'

'Yes?' Obviously he gave himself leave to doubt that, but she closed her lips firmly against further comment. She would not plead; if he chose not to accept her assurances, then she didn't really care.

But when he had gone she found she did care, she cared very much indeed, and when she considered the matter further she could understand how he was feeling. If the positions had been reversed, could she have so easily believed in his innocence? All those late evening meetings, the business dinners would have made the perfect covering for an affair.

The day was the longest of her life. Not even those few desperate days before they married had caused her such anguish. She couldn't think what to do with herself. At one time she went so far as to ring the number of the college and ask if she could speak to Justin. By great good fortune the caretaker assured her that Mr Booth wasn't in the college and she replaced the receiver on his offer to pass on a message. What a stupid thing to do; if the janitor should by chance recognise her voice...

All afternoon she worked in the kitchen, cooking meat, fruit tarts, biscuits, several cakes and a currant loaf, all in a desperate attempt to keep her mind occupied.

It was after eight when she heard the sound of a key in the lock and Adam came in. He glanced at her once, threw his case on to the sofa and slumped on to a chair, sighing, lying back with his eyes closed in a gesture of utter weariness. He opened his eyes, looking at her with an expression she could not fathom. 'Get me a whisky, would you?'

'Of course.' The request surprised and disturbed her; in all the time they had been living together she could not recall an occasion when he'd seemed to have any need for the stimulation of alcohol. Her hands shook as she poured a generous tot. 'What will you have with it, soda or——?'

'No, nothing. Thanks.' He took the glass, raising it to his lips, drinking a little, looking up at her, 'You?' He indicated that she might like a drink but she refused with a swift shake of the head. He reached then for his briefcase and withdrew the envelope which she recognised as the one she had received that morning. 'Well——' he handed it to her '—you can forget about this.'

'Wh...what?' She frowned, uncomprehending. 'What?' she repeated, at the same time reaching blindly for the arm of a chair just behind her and allowing herself to sink into it, her legs threatening to give way beneath her.

'I mean I've cleared the matter up. And you needn't worry any more about it.'

'What happened?' She ought to have felt a surge of relief, vaguely she was aware of that, and was puzzled by the absence of any positive reaction. Perhaps she was still too conscious of the sense of disillusionment and shame, the latter especially acute because Adam was the witness of her degradation.

'When I left here this morning I went straight round to the solicitor in Barnes and——'

'But your meetings...' For the first time she remembered the important discussions in Hamburg, the trip that was to have been their first together before...

'That? Oh, I cancelled the meeting with Hermann; obviously everything else took second place. As I was saying, I went out to Barnes and saw Mr Binks. They tried to fob me off with an assistant but I insisted on seeing the principal, and I left them in no doubt what my next move would be if they persisted in this ridiculous mistake. I think,' he said, his lips twisting wryly, 'he got the point fairly quickly that his client might be risking a suit for substantial damages, so he very speedily arranged a meeting with her. She couldn't make it to the office.' He paused, took another sip from his glass, staring past Nicole to the darkening evening sky. 'She—Mrs Booth—is about to produce her third child. The other two were hanging round her skirts, out of sorts, and the house looked a mess. The poor woman was miserable, and when I began to repeat what I had said to the solicitor she grew quite agitated. I can't say I found it an enjoyable half-hour... However, I was able to convince her that she had made a mistake. She argued a bit at first, but in the end she admitted her informant might have got the wrong name.'

'Oh.' Nicole felt her heart hammering. Her head was aching too, and there was a lump in her throat that threatened to choke her, but she forced herself to speak. 'And you, Adam?' None of her fevered emotions could be discerned in her voice, which was flat, emotionless. 'Are you persuaded that her informant made a mistake?'

He didn't answer that, just turned his head and looked at her very strangely for a few minutes before continuing. 'After that we went back to the lawyer's office for further discussions. He tried to get Booth on the telephone but he was remarkably elusive, so I left to come back to town. It was when I was sitting in the rush-hour traffic that I realised how close I was to the college, and on impulse I turned off and the caretaker directed me up to the studio.'

'Oh?' For no reason she felt a blush envelop her. It was more to do with the intensity of his scrutiny than any sense of guilt.

'Mmm. Apparently he had just come in, and when I got to the top floor he was there. I recognised him, of course.' Her blush deepened and he flicked his eyes away to the glass in his hand; he swirled the amber liquid round a few times then drained it and replaced it on the table. 'He ought to have had the letter from Binks, but for some reason it hadn't reached him. I suppose it's stuck in a cubby-hole somewhere waiting for him to pick it up. Strikes me he's the sort of man who rarely sleeps in the same bed twice. In any event, he got the shock of his life when I explained the reason for my visit and he...more or less corroborated what you told me...'

'More or less...' Anger swept over her in an explosive wave. 'How could he...?'

'Calm down. He confirmed that you and he had never had the kind of relationship his wife was claiming.'

'You're very reluctant to admit it.' Her voice rose as she threw the accusation at him. Her anger included him; she was overwhelmed by that and by a feeling of such desolation...

'I'm sorry if that's how it seems. But shall we finish this story? I'll be glad when it's over and then maybe we can forget it.' His manner suggested that would not be easy. 'Booth told me that you and he had never slept together, but he did confirm he was having an affair with another student, older than you. Helen something...'

'Helen Davidson.' Now that was strange, she had seen Helen on the stairs one day; she had looked upset, but when she had mentioned it to Justin he'd appeared as puzzled as she was.

'Something like that.'

Nicole raked a hand through her hair, and her lips trembled. 'Well, at least I'm off the hook. Thank you for all you've done. I'm sorry you were so involved; it must have been degrading for you.'

'I didn't enjoy it.' His face still wore that peculiar expression. It wasn't that she expected him to feel euphoric, but he might have let her see that he was relieved. And pleased. It wouldn't kill him to show that he was pleased, that his trust in her had been vindicated. She half turned.

'Have you eaten yet?'

'No.' He shook his head. 'No, I had a cheese roll and a cup of coffee about lunchtime.'

'But you must be starving. I've been cooking all afternoon.' She gave a little laugh which could have lightened the atmosphere. 'I can easily——'

'There was something else . . .'

She had reached the door and some instinct caused her to reach out for the handle. A wave of nausea swept over her, reminding her that she had barely eaten since breakfast and that now she felt quite faint. 'Wh . . . what do you mean?' The expression on his face made her nervous. Something else—what could he mean? He was holding a couple of sheets of paper towards her. She let go of the doorknob and took a step towards him. But he released the papers before she was ready and one of them fluttered on to the floor. She bent towards it, scrabbling with her fingers.

Then, when she saw the figure so skilfully sketched on the thick white drawing paper, she felt all the colour drain from her cheeks. For the face, even the attitude were unmistakable. It was Nicole Minter who was lying on the couch in that abandoned pose, lying back and laughing into the face of the artist; she could even remember when Justin had asked her to run her fingers through her hair, to encourage it to fall in disordered waves about her face. 'Come on now, love, give it a bit more pizazz.' And laughingly she had pouted in the most hilariously provocative way possible. He had captured that look in a few clever lines, a little discreet shading; the face laughing at her from that piece of paper was the one she saw in the mirror every day, right down to the sprinkle of tiny freckles the hot weather had brought to the bridge of her nose.

But the rest was a figment of Justin's imagination. The length of leg, the full curve of bosom, the flat stomach and slender waist, the naked body had been drawn with the same eye for intense detail as had been used on the face, and would be capable of fooling anyone who didn't know her intimately.

The other sheet still clutched in her hand, she straightened it out, knowing, with a sense of hopelessness, what she would find. This time the subject was portrayed face down on the couch; the same face looked out provocatively from the tangle of curls, the lines of one raised leg and arched foot seeming to issue a more definite invitation.

A sob escaped her lips, and she looked across through a blur of tears. 'I just don't believe this.'

'I don't imagine you do. I don't suppose you imagined for a minute he would be careless enough to leave things like this lying around.'

'Not *that*.' With the back of her hand she wiped the tears from her face. 'I don't know what Justin meant by this... I... I certainly never posed for him like this.'

'No?' He seemed not to care, just took his briefcase and rose wearily to his feet. 'Well, let's leave the matter for now, shall we? I feel I've had as much emotional upheaval as I can handle for one day. Oh, you mentioned food, but I think I'll get myself a glass of milk and some bread and cheese. I'll eat it in my bedroom.' He brushed past her, through the hall and into his room, reappearing while she was still standing with the sketches in her hand, trying to understand what was happening.

'Are you all right?' He paused, then, when she nodded, went into the kitchen. She heard the clink of glass, the soft thud of the refrigerator door. Barely conscious, she followed, covered the food she had cooked earlier and began to put the dishes away.

'Goodnight, Nicole.' She didn't notice the concern in his voice, nor the look he gave her before he turned away.

'Damn you, Justin Booth.' When she was alone she gave a subdued sigh, picked up the sketches and tore them into pieces, throwing them into the waste disposal and waiting while they were further shredded. Then, she walked into her bedroom and closed the door.

Sleep would be impossible, she knew that. When she emerged from the shower she felt more wide awake than ever as she paced the floor, back and forward, back and forward till her mind was still more confused.

And then it seemed to clear miraculously, and she was struck with this blindingly simple solution. There was one way she could convince Adam that she hadn't been playing around with Justin. Or anyone else, come to that. She owed it to him; she owed it to herself. Besides, it had been a longing deep inside her for ages, an obsession she had been ashamed to admit.

It took just a few moments to get ready. A whole shelf of creams and potions were at her disposal and now was the moment to use them. If ever.

Her eyes were glittering feverishly as she slipped the satin nightdress over her shoulders, tweaking one of the narrow straps so the material lay smoothly against the creamy skin. One last look in the glass confirmed what she already knew; she could feel it in the excited knot at the pit of her stomach, in the seductive slither of material against her breasts, the fall of her auburn hair about her shoulders, the languid, shadowy look on her eyes— all confirmed that she was set on seduction.

A gleam of light still showed under his door, but there was no reply when she tapped. Her heart was bounding fit to escape from her chest when she turned the handle and stepped inside. And there he was, lying across the bed, dressed only in silk pyjama trousers, the steady rise and fall of his chest telling her she was too late.

There was a melting sensation in her chest as she stood looking down at him, a pain as she saw the fan of dark lashes on the cheekbones, a faint shadowing of beard on his chin. How on earth . . . ? She reached out a finger to riffle across the scatter of silky hair on his chest, shuddering with the strength of her own reaction. How could she ever have imagined that she didn't want him? Right now, this minute, it seemed he was the only thing in the world she did want.

He stirred then, eyelids fluttering briefly as if he might wake; his hand came up to touch hers, but as she froze he turned on to his side, frowning as he muttered something that she couldn't quite hear.

Instantly she turned away, moving silently in an excess of anxiety that he might wake and she would be discovered. She refused to admit to any sense of rejection or disappointment. It could, after all, have been so much worse. If he had wakened but shown little interest in her reason for being in his room, how much more humiliating that would have been.

She stood for a moment, her hand on the doorknob, trying to cope with the sudden awareness of her emptiness, then, as she sighed deeply, he spoke again. Indistinctly. The word could have been anything really, and it was idiotic to pretend that her husband was murmuring her name in his sleep. It would be fatally easy to find that, having married for convenience, she was now so madly in love with him that she was prepared to deceive herself that some of her passion was returned.

CHAPTER NINE

NICOLE was grilling bacon and had water ready to poach eggs when Adam appeared in the kitchen next morning. One searching glance and she directed her attention back to the pan. 'Good morning.' She responded to his greeting when she judged her voice was under control. 'I thought, as you didn't eat much yesterday, I would cook you a decent breakfast. Grapefruit's ready.' She nodded towards the table. 'If you would care to start.'

'I do feel a bit empty.' He settled himself in his seat and shook out the pages of the paper. 'You sleep all right?' Although her back was to him she sensed his eyes boring into her.

'Mmm. I was sure I wouldn't, but in the end I did. Woke early, though.' She turned, flourishing the bacon slice. 'You?' she enquired pleasantly.

'Out like a light.' He finished the fruit and pushed the dish away. 'And I got this feeling...' He paused while she pushed a plate in front of him. 'That looks good. Thank you. I got this feeling that someone came into my room last night.' Now his eyes held hers, wouldn't let go. 'You?'

'Yes.' She reached blindly for the coffee-pot and began to pour. 'I did go into your room. But I knocked first.'

'That's all right, then,' he said sardonically before applying himself to eating his breakfast. 'Any special reason for such an unexpected call?'

'No. Well . . . yes. I still had this feeling that you didn't believe me about . . .' She shrugged, turning so her blazing cheeks were hidden from him. 'You know . . . about those sketches and . . .'

'Listen, Nicole, I thought about it a bit too, though I can't pretend it kept me awake all night. And I realise I have no right either to approve or disapprove. As you've said on more than one occasion——' he wiped his mouth with his napkin, '—we don't have that kind of marriage.'

It was ridiculous that she should have such a sense of anticlimax and betrayal. Surely his acceptance of their position was what she wanted, only . . . She watched him push back his chair and stand. 'Surely you want another cup of coffee?' It seemed impossible that he was going when they had so much still to talk over. At least, she wanted to . . .

'I'm sorry, Nicole, I should have said—I'm off to Germany this——'

'Germany?' She felt abandoned, betrayed.

'Yes, I ought to have mentioned . . . I made some early calls and Hermann can spare a couple of hours. Remember I had to cancel yesterday?'

She didn't answer that. What did he expect her to say, for goodness' sake—that she didn't remember? Besides, he was merely rubbing it in, reminding her just how much trouble she had caused. She waited, hoping, half hoping at least, that he might repeat his impulsive invitation, that he might suggest that she grab a jacket and join him but . . . she couldn't wait any longer. 'When will you be back?' Her voice was dull, listless.

'As soon as possible. I don't enjoy this life on the wing, you know. Besides,' his manner eased a little, 'I've been promising that we'll make that trip down to Gloucester pretty soon. I'd like us to get settled, then I plan to start delegating work so I'll have more time.' He glanced at his wrist watch. 'I must get on, I can't afford to miss this flight, but I'll do my best to get back this evening. Certainly I'll be back for tomorrow's affair.'

They had been invited to a reception at the home of an important international banker, an event Adam had been very insistent that they should attend. 'You've bought yourself a dress?'

'Yes.' Was it just three days ago? Since then she felt she had lived a whole lifetime of exhausting emotions. 'Yes, on Tuesday.'

'Mmm. What colour, is one allowed to ask?'

'Oh, a glorious kind of pink. Overlaid with layers of grey. Cost the earth.'

'Sounds promising.' He bent his head and kissed her cheek briefly, the amber-flecked eyes blazing for a second before he turned away. 'Look——' he was fiddling with his briefcase '—why don't you go down to your grandparents for the day? I would rather that than think of you here on your own.'

'I might,' she said, knowing that she wouldn't. She spoke to them daily on the telephone and she knew they were both well and happy. Besides, she read into his remark that he was anxious to get her away from London and all its attendant temptations, but there *were* none. When he had gone she was able to assess the situation and to admit that as far as Justin was concerned there were none; she had little inclination to see him. The beginning of term, still four weeks away, would be all too soon.

Which took her directly to last night's irrational behaviour. She couldn't understand what had pos-

sessed her, to go into Adam's room all done up like
Delilah out on the tiles. Hysterical, really. No
reason to go to such extremes just to prove to Adam
she was pure as the driven snow. It was a blessing
that he had fallen asleep before she had got there.
If she kept on repeating that, she might have a
chance of convincing herself.

Nicole took a step away from the mirror and held
her breath. Impossible to believe that this was an
honest reflection. This new hairstyle…she touched
a tentative hand to the cascade of curls that seemed
to have escaped from the cottage loaf arrangement
on the top of her head. And the rinse had
heightened the burnished chestnut colour. It looked
good, she approved of herself, and it was a longish
time since she had been able to do that whole-
heartedly.

Slowly she turned, fascinated by the way the light
material drifted dreamily out from her body,
wrapped itself about her before swaying back into
the elegant folds. A distinct hint of Ginger Rogers;
she had seen an old film recently and the dresses
had moved in the same gossamer way. It was cut
straight across the neck in front, but dipping to a
V at the back. She picked up the huge filmy wrap
that completed the outfit, and threw it round herself
so the pink marabou made a delicious frame for
her face.

She looked as excited as a child waiting for Santa
Claus, and she wrinkled her nose in an effort at
restraint. Unsuccessfully, for she was fascinated by
her eyes, brilliant and flashing, emphasised by
discreet applications of plum and brown shadowy
powders, slightly slanted by a touch of pencil at

each corner. Her mouth, smeared and glossed with pink and amber, trembled in self-deriding amusement until she was interrupted by a knock at the door.

'Nicole, it's almost time to leave.'

'Yes, I'm coming.' A moment to add another touch of perfume to her wrists; he had brought her a flagon of a new exotic scent from his Hamburg trip. She picked up her evening bag and went to the door. She couldn't ignore her heart, which was behaving in the most irrational way, thumping wildly against her chest so that she was grateful for the concealing folds of her wrap.

When she threw back the door he was turning away, but he paused before swinging back to look at her. For a longish time he looked. Or so it seemed to her. With her heart beating so violently it was difficult to calculate the passage of time. And it seemed he paid little attention to the dress that had cost him a small fortune, concentrating instead on her face. He looked at her hair then . . . back to her face, her mouth. Tension rose inside her till she was forced in some way to break it, and she turned, whirling round so her skirt belled out before settling back in drifting calf-length scallops.

'Well?' In her own ears her voice was breathless, expectant. 'What do you think? Do you like it?' But she was barely capable of hearing his reply; she was much too involved with how he looked in the plain black barathea and white shirt worn tonight under a fancy embroidered waistcoat and with a floppy black silk tie. His skin was tanned and healthy as if he spent his days swimming and scuba-diving instead of shut up in some dreary boardroom in a tower block. He was strapping a platinum watch about his wrist but his eyes never moved from her face; she had an absurd longing to put out a finger, to touch his hair as it fell in a dark swathe on to his forehead, but before she could free a hand he smiled, that brilliant, intoxicating invitation which she had seen so seldom since they married, and he leaned towards her.

'Is one allowed to kiss?' She felt his lips, cool, firm, press against her cheek, though they were removed before her instinct to turn, to search for his mouth could be realised. 'You look stunning, Nicole.' He pulled back. 'And you smell pretty good, too.' He raised one eyebrow. 'Romeo?' It was the name of the latest designer perfume, one she had never heard of until he had produced it on his return from Germany.

Yes, I adore it.' But really, it was the smell of *him* that intoxicated her, a tangy, potent mix of shaving things and the cologne he used. She was so affected that she barely noticed the small box he was holding out towards her.

'For me?' Colour was rushing into her face; it was so obvious that that shape box could contain only one piece of jewellery.

'Who else? I hope you like it.' His voice was so matter-of-fact that for a split second she wondered if she could have made a mistake, but then she pressed the tiny button and looked down at the blaze of diamonds.

'Oh, Adam, I can't...' Unaccountably her eyes filled with tears, and she looked up with a faint shake of her head.

'Of course you can. I should have seen to it before, but what with one thing and another...' He took the ring from the box, caught her hand

and slipped the ring on above the plain wedding band. 'Hmm. Fits, at least. How do you like it?'

'It's...well——' she smiled faintly '—I can't think of a word that's suitable. Gorgeous, exotic, much too good for me.' She tried a joke. 'But I adore it.'

'Good. I'm glad of that. It suddenly occurred to me you ought to have an engagement ring. People will expect it.' She felt slightly crushed. 'I stopped over in Amsterdam to buy it. I took a risk on your liking diamonds.'

'I do.' She held out her slender hand, enjoying the fiery glitter, pleased that she had taken time for a professional manicure, that her pink-tipped fingernails were worthy of such a costly jewel. 'I've never seen such a gorgeous ring.'

'A pink diamond.' This explained something that she had noticed: that this stone gleamed with a softer light than most. 'I wanted something a bit different, and when you mentioned you would be wearing pink this evening... The dress...' he cast a brief glance over her '...from what I can see of it, is a triumph. Is a preview allowed or must I wait till later?'

'Did you say the driver was downstairs?' She raised an eyebrow, smiled a relaxed but still excited smile. Something was happening between them, wonderful, intoxicating; she was holding her breath.

'Yes, yes, he is.' He smiled faintly, leaned forward. Again she felt the touch of his cheekbone against hers. He stepped away from her towards the door. 'Pity,' he said with an enigmatic look.

He seemed to know such a lot of people, that was one of the first things that struck her. There were greetings from all sides and he appeared to feel quite at home in the glittering assembly which she still found slightly overwhelming. Faces about them well known in all walks of life—media folk, politicians, at least one actor who had been elevated to the peerage—all much more at home in this exotic setting than Nicole Minter would ever be.

The house itself was like something from a lush film of a royal dynasty, with a staircase that swept up from a huge marble hall, circular and with alcoves for life-size classical statues. Women, beautiful and not so beautiful, youngish and no longer young at all, dripping with jewels, strolled about sipping from the tulip-shaped glasses of champagne, nibbling exotic mouthfuls from the trays of lavish canapés.

'Darling, come and meet...' She lost count of the times Adam used the endearment, and after hearing it so often she stopped blushing, began to enjoy it, to respond in a way she hoped would be provocative.

'Didn't realise you were married, old boy.' One middle-aged acquaintance surveyed her approvingly through a monocle, speaking in the strangulated upper-class voice Nicole thought had been extinct for years. 'What d'y'mean by hiding her away now, tell me?'

'What did you say his name was?' She had a fit of the giggles when they moved away and had a moment to themselves.

'He's Sir Dennison Berens. And a very important man, so be nice to him.'

'I was.' She was still laughing, but she frowned a little when she saw again what she had noticed earlier, that his attention was not entirely on what they were saying.

He was looking for someone. Oh, not in an obtrusive way, in fact he was being extremely casual about it; every few minutes his eyes would search the room, then come back to what was being discussed with no hint of any other interest. She had no idea who he might be so anxious to meet—probably some business associate. Inwardly she sighed. It seemed people like him never left the world of wheeling, dealing and high finance behind.

But she had almost forgotten about that when they were absorbed by a group of people, mostly about Adam's age, friends who hadn't met for some time and who consequently had lots of catching up to do.

'I had no idea Adam was married.' Cleo, the small, dark woman standing next to Nicole smiled. 'Such a surprise—a pleasant one,' she added as if afraid of being misunderstood. 'It was time you found yourself a wife,' she included him briefly in the conversation before turning more intimately to Nicole. 'You're still in the honeymoon stage, I would guess.'

'Almost.' Nicole was pleased with her own reaction; she didn't even blush, just smiled ruefully and shrugged. 'Married about nine weeks ago.' She sipped from her glass. 'How long have you all known each other?'

'Oh . . . ages. At least, Edward——' she nodded in the direction of her husband, a fair, cheerful-looking man of medium height now engaged in an animated boisterous conversation with Adam '—Edward and Adam went to Haileybury together, then on to Cambridge; that's where I met up with them.'

'I see.' Nicole felt a sudden stab of sheer envy for these people who shared so much. 'All you bright people must have a lot in common.'

'I wasn't one of the bright ones. I scraped in, had to work like mad to get a mediocre degree. Edward was pretty good, but Adam left most of us standing. He really was the most brilliant student of his year, and what he's done since only confirms that. After all, most of us had the help and support of families; he had to make it on his own. If we'd had a vote he would have come out man most likely to succeed. But votes like that are usually the kiss of death; just as well it was never taken.'

'Mmm. He told me he felt he had to prove himself.'

'Well . . . he was brilliant, but I must confess I'm surprised he went into the City. In those days I would have thought the academic life would have been where he would set his sights. But of course that business——' She bit off her words and turned to her husband with a demand for a cigarette. 'Sorry about this.' She puffed and blew the smoke away. 'I've tried time and again to give up, but I can't. Even when I was pregnant——'

'Oh, you have children?'

'Just one, unfortunately. Joelly was born the year after we came down, before we were hammered so insistently about the dangers of smoking in pregnancy. We're dying for another baby, but Edward says we can't have one till I give up the weed.' She looked round for an ashtray and stubbed out the end. 'So things are getting slightly desperate; we really want to produce an heir for this——' She broke off quite suddenly, her expression changing from one of detached amusement to something much more difficult to define as she stared at a group of people who had just come through the wide doors of the reception-room. Nicole saw her glance towards her husband, sending some kind of signal. But he was too involved in what was being said and it was Adam who intercepted her glance, his attention moving instantly from her towards the group now drifting down the room towards them.

There were five of them, two women walking behind and partly obscured by the three men, two tall, rather fleshy, the third short and stout, speaking loudly and gesticulating with the cigar held in podgy fingers.

'Nicole,' Cleo's smile was slightly hectic, 'as you're so keen on art, why don't we go and have a look at the gallery? Lord Melrose has a fabulous collection of Impressionists, and...' The words registered only faintly with Nicole; she was watching the rapt though covert attention Adam was paying to the party approaching. Now she could see that one of the women, handsome and elegant, was about forty, the other small and slender, ten years or so younger. She was wearing a dress in some shimmery gold material that almost matched her hair. And she was strikingly, stunningly beautiful. It gave Nicole an ache just to look at her, the kind of feeling she got when she looked at a perfect work of art.

There was a faint smile on the woman's face, a smile which faded abruptly when she turned her head, attracted perhaps by the intensity of Adam's scrutiny. Something happened to her then; there was a pained intensity about that single brilliant glance, as if the anguish of the world was suddenly laid bare. A look that was abruptly quenched, but for a split second her beauty was crumpled and a little tattered.

Adam was more careful. Nicole took that in, and just as immediately knew that this was the person he had been waiting, watching for. Her heart felt like a stone in her chest as she watched the scene unfold.

Edward, who had dried in the midst of a story, was the first to make a move, going forward to the woman, grasping her hands, pulling her close and kissing her cheek. 'Linda, by all that's strange.' He held her at arm's length. 'And looking as wonderful as ever.'

'Hello, Edward.' The woman smiled, her self-possession entirely restored. 'Hello, Adam.' To him a hand was extended; he took it and stood looking at her without speaking till she moved on, was introduced to the others who were strangers to her.

'And this——' somehow Adam was at her side, fingers were on her arm '—is my wife Nicole. Darling, Lindy Veronese. We were at Cambridge together.'

Lindy. Nicole moved her frozen lips into a smile. That was obviously his own name for her. To the others she was Linda, and the small slip was more revealing than an outright confession. She felt sick, though her lips continued to smile.

Nicole turned to Cleo with the intention of taking up her suggestion about the picture collection, but Cleo had now joined in the animated conversation about old times. It was a subject to which she could add nothing, and no one noticed when she drifted away. Not even Adam, his hand had slipped into his pocket, and he was absorbed by the conversation, though not actually participating.

This, then—numbly she looked at her reflection in the powder-room while she made a few unnecessary repairs to her make-up—this was the woman he had loved so madly all these years. Because of her he had remained a bachelor until König came on to the market with its dual opportunity. An opportunity to add to his already considerable fortune but, more important, the chance to defend himself, to shore up his resolve of a show of indifference to his old love.

But how could she, Nicole Minter—she didn't even think of herself as Nicole Randell—how could she offer any defence against a woman who looked like Linda Veronese? She couldn't; it was as simple as that.

CHAPTER TEN

IN THE car driving home there was silence. It suited Nicole that way; she knew if she had been required to speak she could easily have burst into tears and made a complete fool of herself. It had been a strain pretending she hadn't noticed Adam and Linda talking tête-à-tête when she'd got back to the salon. True, Edward and two of the others had been just a step away, but, while they were engaged in bright laughter, Adam and Linda had been speaking quietly, he looking down into her face with an air of protectiveness which even the distance between them could not minimise.

Cleo's insistence on showing Nicole round the gallery had done little to divert her, though she'd gone through all the motions, made, she supposed, the right comments about the series of glowing Corots, Sisleys and Pissarros. Any other time she would have been entranced by such an extensive private collection, but right then they might have been picture postcards.

A little later, her eyes had sought Adam again, and it had been strange that there was so little relief in seeing him now absorbed into the large group, mainly men, and that Linda Veronese seemed to have vanished. As if feeling her eyes on him, Adam had turned, his glass was raised to his lips, and he had stared intently at her over the rim.

'I think we have to go now, Nicole.' Cleo had touched her arm. 'Baby-sitters, you know. We must get together for coffee some time. Been fun meeting you.'

Shortly afterwards they had been ready to leave themselves, and were walking down the wide staircase when they had found themselves face to face with the Veroneses. He was the small, podgy man, the cigar still clutched in his short fingers while his other hand circled his wife's upper arm, more in the manner of gaoler than protector. They had stood for a few minutes talking rather awkwardly, then parted, Nicole almost running down the steps in her anxiety to escape.

Now, being whisked up in the lift, she felt weary to the heart, sighed deeply as she preceded Adam through the door of the flat, kicking off her shoes as she made for the kitchen.

'You making coffee?' Adam had thrown off his jacket, was pulling at his tie, undoing the buttons of his waistcoat and shirt.

'I wasn't thinking of it.' Meaning to be cool and detached, Nicole glanced across at him and felt her heart turn over. Who could feel uninvolved when he looked as he did, hair falling across his forehead, shirt open halfway down his chest? 'But——' her voice shook only a little '—I'll make you one if you like.'

'Thanks. I'm dying for a cup. These receptions are all right but I hate those silly bits and pieces to eat; I'd welcome an honest-to-goodness sandwich for a change.'

'You mean you want me to make one for you now? There's ham or cheese.'

'Ham would be fine.'

As she buttered bread and sliced ham, wrapped in a man-size apron to protect her dress, she felt drained and empty, her mind so totally disengaged that she looked up in surprise when he appeared at her elbow, perched on a corner of the table.

'I hope you're hungry, Nicole.' He reached out for a sandwich and began to munch approvingly. 'Mmm. They're good.'

'What?' She looked from his face to the pile of bread she had cut, and back to his face again with a faint smile. 'Yes, I suppose I have made rather too many.'

'Never mind.' He took another and, reaching up, brought out two cups and saucers. 'They'll do tomorrow. You're going to have coffee, aren't you?'

'No... Oh, well, I suppose I might have a cup.'

'Won't keep you awake?'

'Maybe.' Again that faint smile and shrug. What did it matter? As a rule it wasn't drinking coffee that kept her awake at nights. She took the cup he held out and, picking up the plate of sandwiches, followed him into the sitting-room.

'If there are any left——' he helped himself to another sandwich '——we might have a picnic tomorrow. I think at last I can spare a day to take you down to look at the house.'

'Oh.' Any interest she might have had in his country property seemed to have evaporated.

'You don't sound all that keen.' Suddenly all his buoyancy faded; he looked as tired and dispirited as she felt, yet she had an absurd longing to put an arm round him, to hold and comfort him. 'I suppose you're tired. You didn't enjoy the evening?'

'Of course I didn't.' The banality of his enquiry suddenly incensed her. Did he expect her to enjoy it, that confrontation with his old lover? 'But I imagine you did.' Unexpectedly a sob escaped her throat, and he looked at her through narrowed eyes but didn't respond. 'I suppose...' she choked back her tears '...you must have known you would see *her* there.'

'Her?' His voice held no expression.

'Oh, don't let's pretend, Adam. I knew you were looking for someone, I could see that—oh, I may not be much of a wife but...you can't live with someone even for a short time and not begin to recognise certain signs. You were restless from the moment we arrived.' She paused and his continued silence angered her still more. 'You're not going to deny it, are you? She is...the one you told me about. The one you——'

'I'm not going to deny it; I did know she would be there.' He raised his cup, stared into the black liquid for a moment, then drained it, replacing it carefully on the saucer, and all the while she was looking at him, feeling as if the ground were dropping away under her feet. 'Yes.' He looked at her again. 'Lindy was the girl I wanted to marry.'

There was a long moment of unbearable tension while she waited for him to say more, then the pain became so crushing, so overwhelming that she turned abruptly. 'You might——' she bent to pick up the wrap she had thrown in the direction of a chair '—you might have told me, prepared me.'

'I didn't think you'd notice.'

'And probably didn't care.' She threw the words over her shoulder, then, afraid of tears, ran across the hall and into her bedroom, slamming the door behind her. Only it didn't close because Adam caught it and stood there watching while she threw herself face down on the bed.

'Nicole.' He sat on the edge of the bed and touched her shoulder. 'You're not crying, are you?'

'No, of course not.' She turned so she was lying across the bed, staring up at him, only the brilliance of her eyes contradicting the words. She saw a faint smile on his face.

'Nicole.' He shook his head as if at a slightly naughty child. 'You know, you're still wearing your butcher's apron. It ruins the look of that expensive dress. Stand up so I can take it off.'

Obediently she stood, bowing her head while he undid the ties and lifted it over her head. 'That's better.' He tossed the apron on to a chair and put his hands gently about her waist. 'In case I didn't tell you, you were quite the most beautiful woman there tonight.'

'Please don't patronise me.' His words were the last she wanted to hear; she pulled herself from his grasp, turned and walked to the dressing-table, pulling distractedly at the pins so her hair tumbled about her shoulders. 'Do you think I couldn't see just how you felt about her.' Her mouth trembled when she saw his reflection very close to her.

'And,' he said, his voice very low, 'how did I feel, Nicole?'

For a moment she couldn't think of a reply so she temporised. 'How would any man feel? She's a very beautiful woman.'

'You are more beautiful.'

'Younger, that's all. She's also more sophisticated, with ten times more poise and experience and——'

'And she would never have dreamt of making the kind of sacrifice you did for your grandparents.'

'What?' She frowned, turned round to face him. 'What?'

'You heard.' There was a tortured twist to his mouth. 'Lindy wasn't into self-sacrifice ten years ago and I doubt if she's learned much on the subject in the meantime.'

Nicole gazed at him, her eyes raking his face for some explanation of the words she was hearing. When his hands came out and linked about her waist again she offered no resistance. And none when he held her against him for a brief moment.

'I'd like to tell you all about it, Nicole. I should have told you before but I was . . . I was afraid you might regret our . . . arrangement even more. Please, will you listen to me now?'

She nodded, felt herself being led back to the sitting-room. She sat down on the sofa and waited. First of all he paced the room several times, then, making an effort, he came and sat at the far end of the sofa. She swung round so she could watch his face, curling her feet underneath as she waited for him to begin.

'We met on our very first day at Cambridge. She was wearing one of those wide peasant skirts that were so popular at the time, cream and splashed with brilliant colours round the border. That's how I always remembered her.' Nicole felt a stab of pain deep in her stomach. He had never shown much interest in what she wore. And he was still remembering, if the prolonged silence was anything to go by.

'Well, as I said, we met that first day and I . . . I'll admit it, I fell in love with her immediately. On her side——' he laughed briefly, self-dismissively '—it took a bit longer. Well, in spite of what you might have heard to the contrary, we didn't all instantly jump into bed. For one thing there was a lot of work to do, and for another . . . well, I thought of our relationship as something permanent; there was no reason for such a great hurry. Anyway, things did develop in that direction. When we were in Greece the Easter before the finals things got out of control, and when we got back we rented a tiny flat where we had peace to study as well as . . .' He glanced round and she was shocked by the ravaged expression on his face, longed to scramble forward, to slip a hand into his, lean her head on his shoulder. 'I had more or less been promised a research scholarship subject to my results, and I could see no earthly reason why we shouldn't get married. OK, we wouldn't be well off, but we would manage, and marriage was our long-term plan after all. I had to go up to London for a few days and she decided she would go and speak to her parents about the wedding; she was adamant that she preferred to go on her own instead of waiting till I could go with her, which was what I wanted. Anyway, when I got back she was waiting in the flat, very white.' He shrugged his shoulders, spoke gruffly. 'Then she began to cry and after a lot of hassle she told me she had more or less decided to marry someone else. She had met a millionaire who was crazy about her and she had agreed to marry him. I didn't believe it at first. Knowing how we felt for each other, it seemed impossible, but at last she convinced me—after quite a lot of shouting and accusations—that her mind was made up. She began to pack then, gathering her things together into boxes and cases, and after I had calmed down a bit I went and leant on the bedroom door watching. I felt bitter and, I suppose...rejected. She married the man she wanted; I understand they had a huge wedding, yards of white lace and six bridesmaids, and they left by helicopter for their honeymoon. I must confess she would have had none of that if she had married me.'

'Adam——' Nicole didn't even think; this time she moved close, took his hand and held it against her cheek. 'Oh, Adam, I'm so sorry. So sorry.' She was very close to tears.

'Mmm.' His hand came up and tangled in her hair, rubbing gently, comfortingly. 'I thought I would never recover from that: her going, the cruel things we said. But there, it's over, has been for a long time. And I suppose,' she could sense a smile, faint, rueful, 'it's thanks to Lindy and Mr Veronese that I'm where I am. I could so easily have become an academic. Instead I made up my mind that if money was what it took then surely I could beat him at his own game. And I think I very nearly have, except I think my business ethics are a little more decent. When I knew one of his subsidiaries was sniffing round König, that made me all the more determined to have it. To thwart him, but also because I knew and respected your grandfather and I didn't want him to be ground down in his dealings with them. And, while I don't want to pose as the world's greatest philanthropist, I do try to consider what will happen to the workforce. As it happens we've been able to recruit more staff since I acquired the company and the bonuses are bigger, so I think everyone's happy.'

'I see.' Decisively, reluctantly, Nicole withdrew from him and stood up. 'I'm glad it's all been worthwhile. Thank you, Adam, for telling me about . . . what happened.'

'No.' Now he was standing too, looking down at her with a strange expression, almost tender. 'Thank you, my love.' The words caused a shudder to rub down her spine. 'You can't imagine what it meant to have you beside me today. I . . .' Whatever he had been about to add was stifled by a sigh, a deep, woeful sound that very nearly brought the tears to her eyes again. 'You must be weary, Nicole; don't let me keep you up if you want to go to bed.' And she felt herself dismissed.

Bed. When she reached her room she sighed, looking bleakly at the large double bed. It was the last thing in the world she wanted. At least . . . Oh, damn. The tears were spilling down her cheeks, and with a feeling of sheer desperation she tore off her clothes and went to stand under a cool shower . . . the oldest known remedy for over-excited feelings. Ruefully she looked at her reflection as she pulled off the shower-cap. So why wasn't it working, then?

Even when she was lying in the dark between cool, sweetly scented sheets she knew that sleep would be elusive. An hour later she was still tossing and turning, her body fevered by all kinds of tortured thoughts and tormented by the more easily remedied problem of an enormous thirst.

For a while longer she lay, concentrating her mind on a bottle of lemonade which was waiting in the fridge, and then she threw back the covers and padded barefoot, silent to the kitchen. It was after she had drunk some lemonade and was refilling her glass that she heard music, soft and evocative. She paused by the nearly closed door of the sitting-room, then, placing her hand on the smooth wood, she pushed. A single lamp still burned and Adam was lying in one of the deep armchairs at full stretch, hands crossed under his head, eyes closed so that for a moment she thought he had fallen asleep.

And when he spoke she was so startled that she jumped, spilling some of the lemonade down the front of her nightdress.

'Hello, Nicole. Couldn't you sleep, was the music disturbing you?'

'No, of course not. I just felt restless and thirsty.' She held up the glass and took a step or two further into the room, 'I didn't hear the music till I was in the hall. What's the matter?' She looked up into his face as he got to his feet, seeing none of the signs of stress and strain that she half feared. 'Didn't you feel like sleep either?'

He smiled faintly. 'I'm one of those people who don't need a lot of sleep. Never have. Useful at times, but I understand it makes us difficult to live with. I'm sorry you can't sleep, Nicole.' He came forward, putting his hands on her bare shoulders, and when the strap of her satin nightdress slipped she made no move to fix it. 'Go back to bed.' He bent his head, brushed his mouth against her forehead, then, rather deliberately, released her and turned away.

'What...?' Her heart was hammering now; vaguely she was aware of her reflection in a mirror, a slenderly seductive figure in peach-coloured satin, russet hair cascading down to her shoulders. 'What is that music, Adam?'

'That?' He cast a quick grin in her direction. 'Terribly hackneyed, I'm afraid. A Rachmaninov concerto—used to be a favourite when I was at Cambridge.'

'Oh.' All feeling seemed to drain out of her then. 'Was it...?' She hated herself for asking but the words came in spite of herself. 'Was it one of her favourites? Linda's?' She held her breath as he looked down in surprise, none of the anger or even the irritation that might have been expected.

'Linda's?' He shook his head, one swift move, absolute in its finality. 'I shouldn't think so. I don't think she had much interest in music; maybe a bit of jazz, that's all.'

'Oh.' Some explanation was called for. 'I thought maybe it reminded you...of her.'

'No. I suppose speaking to Edward and Cleo made me feel a bit nostalgic, that's all. Nothing to do with Lindy, though.'

Lindy. Again! Jealousy stabbed through her, tearing, destructive.

'Come on, now.' Suddenly brisk and businesslike, he reached out to switch off the music and light, and they were left in the still soft gloaming. 'It's nearly one and you're quite right, time all decent people were in bed. Besides, I know you youngsters need all the sleep you can get.'

He draped his arm about her shoulder but she shrugged it off in sudden fury, turning to face him. 'Is *that* how you see me? Like some child who's been allowed to stay up late? Is it?' She was very nearly shouting. 'Do you realise I'll be twenty-one next month, that I've had the vote for three years? I get furious——' she had over-reacted and she knew it, losing her temper at something trivial '—at your constant refusal to treat me as other than a foolish sixteen-year-old.'

'How——' his voice was deeper, at the same time tense and throbbing, more sensual than she had ever known it; she could almost *feel* his fingers tracing delicious paths across the most tender vulnerable parts of her body '—how can you expect me to cope with this situation otherwise?' The words were the very last she expected to hear, and for a moment she was unable to absorb their significance.

'Wh...what?' She stared up as he took a step closer. 'I...I don't know what you mean.' But she was beginning to, only it was so crazy she dared not allow...

'I mean, my dear wife,' he said, taking the glass from her hand, setting it down on a table then, linking his hands about her waist, pulling her against him, 'that the only way I can control things is by persuading myself that you are a sixteen-year-old, that I'm thirty-one and that any...close relations between us would be hard to justify. Only, it's becoming increasingly difficult when my eyes tell me the exact opposite; that you're a beautiful and exciting woman.'

Passion rose inside her like a tidal wave, and when his face came down to hers this time there was no brief, chastely deposited kiss on her forehead. His mouth brushed seductively, his tongue described the most delicate tracery on her inner lips and his fingers were caressing through the slippery folds of satin.

And she, sense and restraint abruptly jettisoned, was blissfully indulging her long repressed feelings, was exploring his chest, quivering fingers finding delight in the messages from his hammering pulses, the warm, silken skin, the rough brush of hair.

'Nicole?' It was a hoarse, breathy query, and her reply was a faint moan, a fevered look from beneath heavy eyelids, drooping lashes; then she was being carried through to her bedroom, shadowy in the light of a single lamp, and was laid down.

'Nicole.' When he stood up there was the same enquiry. 'You're sure?'

Her reply was to kneel on the bed, drag the filmy nightdress over her head and toss it away from her. 'So very sure,' she replied. Her fingers were reaching out for the buttons of his shirt.

'I *think* I can just about manage that.' Adam grinned at her briefly and a moment later lay down beside her, mouth to mouth, thigh to thigh. They watched each other through barely open lids. 'I can hardly believe this is happening.' His hand cradled the full taut curve of her breast, thumb moving gently over the rosy peak.

Nicole shuddered against him, burying her face against his shoulder as she tried to cope with intense joy, but control was impossible, and his name, a flood of endearments came to her lips. 'Adam!' She strained to get closer to him. 'I can't think what took you so long.'

*   *   *

In the dawn she stirred slightly, reached out a hand and encountered warm firm flesh. Her eyes shot open in disbelief and encountered a similar semi-shocked expression which melted at once into a smile of beguiling tenderness. 'You can't understand——' a hand brushed a coppery wisp of hair from her forehead, trailed down her cheek and came to rest against her throat '—why I took so long, is that what you said?'

'What?' Her mind was so distracted that her words of the previous night were almost obliterated from her memory.

'You said——' an arm snaked about her waist, pulled her close so she could hear the agitated tattoo of his heart, knew that her own pulses were beginning to sing in response '—that you couldn't——'

'Oh, yes, I remember.' Her lips on his stifled an immediate reply, but after a few minutes he spoke huskily.

'Don't you realise, I've been struggling against my own feelings since almost the first day we met, afraid even to touch you?'

'I'm just asking, what kept you?' Her lips kept moving against his, distractingly.

'You, *you* can ask that? When you told me you didn't even like me?'

'Oh?' *Had* she said that? Had she been so stupid as to suggest... There was just the vaguest memory... 'That was nothing.'

'Nothing?' he jeered. 'I have an in-built aversion to making love to a woman who says she doesn't like me. Especially when I happen to be married to her. Still more when I'm mad for her.'

'Oh, you.' She grinned, aimed a glancing blow at his chin, then immediately followed up with a delicate exploration of fingers. 'You need a shave, you know that?'

'I'll go and shave now if, *if* you promise not to move from the spot till I come back.'

'No, don't.' Her arms tightened. 'I don't want you to leave me.'

'I don't have the energy.' He laughed, then grew more pensive. 'Tell me, when did you first decide that you didn't dislike me as much as you first thought?'

'Oh, a long time ago.' Nicole sighed deeply as she rubbed her cheek lightly against his. 'I might have felt like doing something about it sooner if...' she bit her lip fiercely, regretting that she had brought up the subject so soon '...if you hadn't told me about Linda. Knowing that you were still in love with a woman you had known years before, well...'

'Is that the impression I gave?'

'You *know* you did.' She thumped him playfully on the chest. 'That's what you said.'

'Weren't you even *listening* to me a little while ago?' He nibbled at her ear. 'Didn't you hear me telling you that I was crazy for you, that I loved you madly and forever?'

'And did you mean it, Adam?' She sounded young and uncertain. 'Or were you saying what...what I suppose people do say in...in these circumstances?'

'I mean it. Lord, how——' he paused to give the word emphasis '—*how* I mean it! I know now that I've been waiting all my life for you. And I can't understand why she cast such a long shadow. I think maybe it was because of how it happened. It made the break so much worse; it was all so bitter.'

'I can see that. And now...' She felt very tentative about asking but she had such an urgent need to know. 'Now do you feel you're getting her out of your system at last?'

'Good heavens, woman, haven't the last few hours demonstrated as much? Do you think I would have had the stamina if even a corner of my mind were on something else?'

'Good.' She snuggled against him, sighing with sheer pleasure. 'I can't even begin to tell you how happy I am.'

'Show me.' His fingers were under her chin, tilting her face up, his eyes as exciting as the exploration of his hands. 'Show me,' he whispered against the corner of her mouth. 'Show me how happy you are.'

Much later she struggled back to life, gasping in mock horror when she saw that it was almost ten o'clock. She turned round to warn Adam and found she was alone. But even before she could move the door opened and he appeared with a tray and tea-things. Bare-legged, he was dressed in a dark blue towelling robe, and when he sat on the edge of the bed, lowered his head to hers, she could smell toothpaste and shaving soap, the clean shower-fresh scent of him.

'In case I didn't make myself clear earlier——' he handed her a cup of tea, laughing at her efforts to cover herself with the sheet pulled high about her '—I love you. Adore you. And meeting Linda last night served only to emphasise a fact I was well aware of. I felt nothing for her, just a faint sadness that what she wanted all those years ago has eluded her. And she hasn't even made her husband happy, for he wants the one thing she finds she cannot give him.'

'You mean...'

'Children. Sons. He is almost desperate to have someone to hand things on to. But it seems it hasn't happened. They've been to every medical expert in the Western world...'

Nicole sipped her tea, surprising herself with a pang of sympathy for the other woman. Adam spoke again.

'Oh, and that brings me on to something else. I never really believed you were having an affair with... with him. Even before last night.' He laughed softly as he saw the colour run up under her skin, then leaned forward and kissed the tip of her nose. 'I was just so madly jealous...'

'You were?' She knelt on the bed, shameless now about the covers falling away. 'I'm glad.' Her fingers began to slide beneath his robe but were caught and held securely.

'Don't.' He rose and held out a hand for the tray. 'We haven't time.'

'Haven't time?' she echoed in tones of disbelief. Did he mean he was going to hurry off to some meeting or...?

'And might I suggest you think of getting up and doing some packing?'

'Packing?' Her brain was still half dazed; it had been a time of such wonder and delight that she... 'But I thought you said something about going down to look at your new house, for the day, I think you said, and...'

'We'll take a raincheck on that. I'm taking you off somewhere we can be on our own. I managed to get some seats on an afternoon flight.'

'Where?' She was suddenly breathless with excited anticipation, 'Where are we going, Adam?'

'I suddenly made up my mind——' he put down the tray and held her as she stepped from the bed into the circle of his arms '—that the next time we made love it would be to an orchestra of crashing waves, a choir of seabirds and cicadas.' The humorous twist of his lips invited her to share his amusement, 'And so we're booked on a flight to Jamaica.'

'Jamaica?' Her voice was dreamy and sentimental. 'Oh, Adam. Where we were married!'

'Yes,' he said with amused dryness. 'And where you wore that special wedding dress just to show what you thought of men who force young girls into marriage.'

'Mmm.' She laughed softly. 'Sorry about that. I was making a statement about the white slave trade; can't think why right now.'

'So,' he smiled at the provocatively fluttered eyelashes, 'you'll come?'

'Try to stop me.' She wrapped her arms about his neck. 'All I object to is that one condition.'

'Mmm?'

'You said you wouldn't make love till we got there.'

'I made up my mind.'

'Really?' She moved her hands, slipped them inside his robe, moved her hands across the skin.

'You're determined on that?' she breathed against his ear.

'Quite.' He caught at her hands. 'Quite... quite...determined.'

'Sure?' She nibbled at his earlobe, laughing when a stifled groan came from his lips.

'Almost sure,' he managed to say before capitulating totally.

4 FREE

Romances
and 2 Free gifts
-just for you!

Now you can enjoy all the heartwarming emotions of true love for FREE! Discover the uncertainties and the heartbreak, the motions and tenderness of the modern relationships found in Mills & Boon Romances.

We'll send you 4 captivating Romances as a free gift from Mills & Boon, plus the chance to have 6 Romances delivered to your door every single month.

Claim your FREE books and gifts overleaf.

An irresistible offer from Mills & Boon

Here's a personal invitation from Mills & Boon Reader Service, to become a regular reader of romance. To welcome you, we'd like you to have four books, a CUDDLY TEDDY and a special MYSTERY GIFT absolutely FREE.

Then each month you could look forward to receiving 6 more Brand New Romances, delivered to your door, post and packing free! Plus our Free newsletter featuring author news, competitions and special offers.

This invitation comes with no strings attached. You can cancel or suspend your subscription at any time, and still keep your free books and gifts.

Its so easy. Send no money now. Simply fill in the coupon below and post it to - **Mills & Boon Reader Service, FREEPOST, PO Box 236, Croydon, Surrey CR9 9EL**

- - - - - - - **NO STAMP REQUIRED** - - - - - -

Free Books Coupon

YES! Please rush me my 4 Free Romances and 2 Free Gifts! Please also reserve me a Reader Service Subscription. If I decide to subscribe I can look forward to receiving 6 brand new Romances each month for just £8.70 delivered direct to my door, post and packing is free. If I choose not to subscribe I shall write to you within 10 days - I can keep the books and gifts whatever I decide. I can cancel or suspend my subscription at any time. I am over 18.

Name Mrs/Miss/Ms/Mr _____ EP87R

Address _____

_____ Postcode _____

Signature _____

The right is reserved to refuse an application and change the terms of this offer. Offer expires December 31st 1990. Readers in Southern Africa write to Independent Book Services Pty., Post Bag X3010, Randburg 2125, S.A. Other Overseas and Eire send for details. You may be mailed with other offers from Mills & Boon and other companies as a result of this application. If you would prefer not to share in this opportunity please tick box ☐

Accept 4 Free Romances and 2 Free gifts

• FROM MILLS & BOON •

An irresistible invitation from Mills & Boon Reader Service. Please accept our offer of 4 free romances, a CUDDLY TEDDY and a special MYSTERY GIFT... Then, if you choose, go on to enjoy 6 more exciting Romances every month for just £1.45 each postage and packaging free. Plus our FREE newsletter with author news, competitions and much more.

Send the coupon below at once to:
Reader Service, FREEPOST, P.O. Box 236,
Croydon, Surrey CR9 9EL

— — — — — — — NO STAMP NEEDED — — — — —

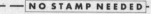

YES! Please rush me my 4 Free Romances and 2 FREE Gifts! Please also reserve me a Reader Service Subscription so I can look forward to receiving 6 Brand New Romances each month for just £8.70, post and packing free. If I choose not to subscribe I shall write to you within 10 days. I understand I can keep the free books and gifts whatever I decide. I can cancel or suspend my subscription at any time. I am over 18 years of age.

Name Mr/Mrs/Miss ————————————————— EP86R

Address ————————————————————————

————————————————————————————

——————————————— Postcode —————————

Signature —————————————————————————

The right is reserved to refuse an application and change the terms of this offer.
Offer expires May 31st 1991. Readers in Southern Africa write to Independent
Book Services Pty., Post Bag X3010, Randburg 2125, South Africa. Other Overseas
and Eire send for details. You may be mailed with other offers as a result of this
application. If you would prefer not to share in this opportunity please tick box ☐

Next month's romances

Each month, you can choose from a world of variety in romance with Mills & Boon. These are the new titles to look out for next month.

THE STEFANOS MARRIAGE Helen Bianchin

THE LAND OF MAYBE Sandra Field

THE THREAT OF LOVE Charlotte Lamb

NO REPRIEVE Susan Napier

SOMETHING FROM THE HEART Amanda Browning

MISSISSIPPI MISS Emma Goldrick

RANCHER'S BRIDE Jeanne Allan

A VINTAGE AFFAIR Elizabeth Barnes

JUNGLE LOVER Sally Heywood

ENDLESS SUMMER Angela Wells

INHERIT YOUR LOVE Sally Cook

WILD CHAMPAGNE Kate Kingston

PORTRAIT OF A STRANGER Helena Dawson

NOT HIS PROPERTY Edwina Shore

Available from Boots, Martins, John Menzies, W.H. Smith, Woolworths and other paperback stockists.

Also available from Reader Service, P.O. Box 236, Thornton Road, Croydon, Surrey CR9 3RU.

Readers in South Africa — write to:
Independent Book Services Pty, Postbag X3010, Randburg, 2125, S. Africa.